Praise for HOW TO RATE A SOULMATE

This is a gem of a book, funny yet full of angst. D.L. Fisher has filled *How to Rate a Soulmate* with some awesome characters. This is a perfect summer read.

—5 stars, Readers' Favorite

Besides being laugh out loud funny, the story entertained with twists and unexpected surprises. I read this book from cover to cover in one sitting—it is a delicious, delightful diversion you won't want to put down!

—K Z Kane, author of *Blindfolded: A True Story*

How to Rate a Soulmate is everything an intelligent romantic comedy should be.

—M. Plets, author of *Kelly: a tale of ould Ireland*

How to Rate a Soulmate is a tasty, uproarious read that you can't put down until you find out if Sara ever finds "the one."

—Lavinia James, author of *At First Sight*

HOW TO RATE A SOULMATE

A Romantic Comedy

D. L. FISHER

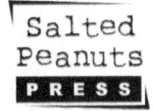
Salted
Peanuts
PRESS

HOW TO RATE A SOULMATE

For more information, please address Salted Peanuts Press, 43633 N. 13th Avenue, New River, AZ 85087.

Book design by Zero Gravity Studios

ISBN: 978-1-7323855-1-1

How to Rate a Soulmate

Prologue

LOOKING FOR A SOULMATE CAN BE EXHAUSTING.

S ARA'S CHERRY WAS POPPED by Derrick. It was the inevitable result of mind-numbing college parties and mistaken identity. After each shot of tequila, Derrick looked more and more like Jon Bon Jovi and less like Pee-wee Herman. Luckily, Sara had little memory of the actual event beyond a few disconnected flash-backs, thanks to the tequila.

Sara's first love was Brad. He was a sensitive artist with long wavy hair who wore t-shirts that said, Save the Whales, and, Trees Are People Too. But no one warned Sara of the horrible truth about Brad: he had Scorpio in his eighth house. This made him a great lay, but also a slut. At his first opportunity, Brad shagged Sara's best friend, Kathy, who had insider knowledge of Brad's prowess. A hideous fight and breakup ensued, with Sara alone again and no best friend to bitch to about it.

Then there was Jim, a clean-cut physical therapist who was roman-tic, caring, and had excellent muscle tone. Things seemed to be going pretty well until Sara began finding mail addressed to Jamie. It wasn't long before a tearful, apologetic Jamie announced that he had a new boyfriend, but they could still be girlfriends.

Sara still blushes when she thinks of Night. Night was a wild man, extreme sports enthusiast, and rode a crotch-rocket that rarely had both wheels on the pavement. While he was not ideal husband material, his extreme gymnastics in the bedroom and his boyish charm made her fall for him hard. Night, however, went off one day to climb Mt. Everest and was now somewhere in Nepal snowboarding down the other side. He hadn't officially broken up with her, but effectively postponed their next date for a few years, breaking Sara's heart nonetheless. Sara never really got over Night.

She could have married Greg. She met him at work. He was as boring as macaroni and cheese, but this was a relief after Night. It was the Internet that did this relationship in. While Sara thought Greg was up late researching his latest solar-powered-weed-eating-robot idea, he was actually "chatting" with the likes of blackleatherbabe and teenhottie. She caught him one sleepless night with his pants down, red-handed, having a nice little chat with spankme2nite.

Sara's enthusiasm for a relationship flagged at this point.

PART I
The Plan

Sara's new boyfriend

Sara looked at the box. The box looked back.

"No one's looking," the box seemed to say. "For pity's sake, open me and stop gaping."

Sara bit her lip in embarrassment.

She remembered hearing somewhere that all mail was routinely x-rayed. She thought of Larry, the mailman. She thought of the mail sorters. She imagined them all gathered around the screen, commenting on her package as it slid through on a conveyer belt.

"Nice shape!" "Looks like an eight-incher." "It's probably hot pink."

"Okay, get a grip," Sara said to herself. "Nobody but me knows what's in this box and what color it is. The mail sorters don't know anything about my discreet, online purchase, except for the dubious return address label. They don't know the flesh-colored ones gave me the creeps because they looked like dismembered members. Besides, I like hot pink. Why am I babbling to myself?"

"Because you haven't gotten a grip yet," said the box.

Sara grabbed the box and was about to tell it to shut up, when she finally got a grip.

She opened the box, and pulled out another box. On it were photos of the hot pink dildo in use.

The photos gave Sara ideas for wielding a dildo she hadn't thought of.

But life was ticking by as Sara stared at photos on a box. She had somewhere to go, and if she was going to get there and try out her new purchase first, she must stop gaping and get on with it.

And so, on to the birthday party

Sara took a deep breath and smoothed her shoulder-length, dyed-to-hide-the-gray-strands auburn hair. She reflected with relief that this was a good hair day. She was meeting friends for a latte. While this sounded like a pleasant idea, Sara was more in a mood to mutilate Barbie dolls.

It was her birthday, and Sara was dangerously close to tears.

She wished she had lived her life differently. If only she could go back nineteen years and start over.

She would go to the gym every day and by now, at age thirty-nine, she would look like Linda Hamilton in *Terminator 2*.

She would use moisturizer faithfully and never squint or frown. She would wear sunscreen and not get a tan. She would eat only raw vegetables and drink carrot juice.

She would shop at Walmart and save money. She would sell her condo at the peak of the real estate bubble, and live in a one-bedroom apartment to save more money. She would invest the extra cash in Apple before the iPhone came out.

She would not waste her youth trying to please a man. She would drive herself mercilessly in her career. She would produce the espionage novel she fancied herself writing during the half hour a day she allowed herself for downtime.

She would read only educational books.

If she had done all that, Sara thought, she'd be sitting pretty now. She'd be happy.

But she had not done any of those things. She was certainly not sitting pretty.

Sara had a good visual going of melting the cone-like plastic Barbie boobs with a lighter, carefully, so they didn't burn but lost their youthful pertness and sagged realistically, when she heard "Happy Birthday!"

"You are the center of the universe darling and this is your day," said a stylishly disheveled man.

Sara slid into a chair with "please shut up" written clearly on her face.

"Ash," she said, "what makes you think I want to flaunt my thirty-ninth birthday in front of a roomful of highly caffeinated cheerful people?"

Ash didn't have an answer for this. He could not imagine being unhappy on his birthday. So he looked at Andi, who was stirring her caramel-whip-frap trying to think of something nice, but not too cheerful, to say.

"It's PMS isn't it?" Andi said. "Murphy's law—the one day you are supposed to be happy, you get PMS."

"I don't have PMS," Sara told her. "I'm merely dealing with the inevitability of my decline into decrepitude."

"Oh, well," Ash perked up, "then you'll be delighted to know we brought a wheelchair so we could take you somewhere special. It's in the van."

"What van?" Sara asked. "Neither of you owns a van."

"I bought it in preparation for our old age," Ash said. "It's my duty as the man in this circle of friends to take care of my aging women. Besides, I can use it for my bookstore."

"Ash, you're finally growing up just in time to decay and die, and what makes you think I need taking care of?" Sara felt her chin tremble. "I'm getting a coffee."

"No," Ash said, "let me darling. It's your birthday. Jeesh, you need some drugs."

"Birthday blues," said Sara while she slumped further into her chair and suffered Ash to get her some drugs.

Ash came back with a triple latte and an iced brownie the size of a small pie. Sara sipped the high-octane mood-enhancer. Here she was, celebrating a birthday she didn't want, biological clock ticking away, no husband, no boyfriend, and relegated to wielding a dildo for sexual satisfaction. Sara was wondering if things could get worse.

"Can you believe that wanker Greg is getting married?" Ash asked Sara, thinking a little healthy anger was better than depression. "What?" he whined to Andi, "stop kicking me."

"Ash, you idiot."

"Greg's getting married?" asked Sara. Her coffee suddenly tasted like plutonium.

Ash, who now figured out he had screwed up, sipped his mocha for all it was worth and hummed a happy little ditty trying to turn Sara's thoughts.

Andi glared at him and told Sara, "Yeah. You know Brittney, the—"

"You mean the overdressed-kiss-ass designer? The overdressed-kiss-ass designer in our freaking office?" Sara hissed through bared teeth, eyes leveled at Andi.

"Well," Andi hesitated, "you didn't still care for Greg, did you?"

"That's not the point." Sara gritted her teeth so hard she corrected the slight misalignment in her bite.

"Listen love," Ash soothed, "Greg's an idiot and you're lucky to be rid of him."

Sara suddenly saw her life as it must look to others: pathetic. The box was right, she did not have a grip at all. She started to tear up but mastered her vulnerability by gritting her teeth again.

"Okay," Andi said, "time for the birthday surprise. Guess where we're taking you?"

"To another planet where thirty-nine-year-old women with thighs full of cottage cheese are actually considered sexually attractive?"

"What are you talking about?" Ash said. "Thirty-nine is the new twenty-nine."

"Either way, it's a baby step away from an unwanted decade change," Sara reminded him.

"Sara, eat your brownie," Andi urged. "You need the endorphins. And your thighs are not fat."

Sara stared at her iced brownie. It had the texture of a fresh dog turd. She sipped her triple latte and thought about cow's teats. The segue here was the milk in her latte.

"I need liposuction," Sara moaned.

"We're taking you to a psychic," Ash blurted out. "It was Andi's idea."

"A psychic? You mean, as in, fortune teller?"

"As in, she's the best psychic around," Andi said. "It took months to get an appointment."

Sara smiled to hide her apprehension. She was secretly worried the psychic would know about the hot pink dildo, which she had used vigorously just before she came to the coffee shop.

"Cheer up love. You have a good forty years ahead of you," Ash reminded her. "You can always hire cabana boys for sex."

"You're entering the best years of your life," Andi said. "All women over forty say that. I can't wait to hear what Celestara tells you."

"The only forty-year-old women who ever say that are celebrities," Sara said, "and they've all had plastic surgery."

The embarrassing past life

"**A**sh, you're such a dork," Sara said. "Are you trying to be a soccer mom?"

"Soccer moms drive SUVs, not vans. Vans are for old fogies like us. I'm going to have it wrapped too. Pictures of books all over it. It'll be brilliant."

"Not one of us has even hit forty yet," Andi pointed out. "Old fogy does not apply to us."

"I'm just trying to go with the flow. Sara is whining about aging so I thought I would too, darling."

"The Einsteinian Relativistic Age Reversal timeline is different for men anyway," Sara said.

"What the bloody hell is that?" Ash asked.

"It's the sudden shift from wanting to be older, to actually getting older and not wanting to. For women it's twenty-five. I figure we get a five-year window of peak opportunity."

"It's not twenty-five for me," Andi said. "I was a bumbling idiot at that age."

"Ditto. I couldn't even speak in complete sentences," said Ash.

"All Brits speak proper English, even when they're two," Sara reminded Ash. "Makes you sound intelligent."

"I am intelligent. And sensitive. I've read Jane Austen. I must say however, that *Pride And Prejudice* was her only decent work."

"Right, if only I could have my thirty-nine-year-old brain and my twenty-five-year-old body," Sara sighed. "On second thought, my brain is generally fried from estrogen dominance. I'm screwed."

Ash slowed down and began scanning addresses in a very nice neighborhood. Sara's heart skipped a beat.

"I'll bet you weren't happy with your twenty-five-year-old body when you were twenty-five," Andi said.

"What's your point?" Sara asked her. "I'd be happy with it now."

"You could join the ranks of celebrities and have plastic surgery," Ash said. "Nip and tuck your way back to your twenties, and keep your aging brain in the process. Ah, here we are darling."

Sara stiffened and her pupils dilated with fear. She was not sure at all she wanted to do this. In fact, she knew she didn't.

Unable to back out now, Sara reluctantly followed her friends to the covered entryway. Ash rang the doorbell.

The door was answered by a middle-aged woman wearing what looked like a galaxy: cosmic colors and filmy layers all swirling and flowing mystically. She was rather plump and comfortable-looking in a maternal sort of way. Then Sara noticed the piercing steel-blue eyes, which were even now probing her secret depths. Sara didn't even know she had secret depths, notwithstanding the pink dildo.

"Ms. Somers," the psychic said, taking Sara's hand. Sara could hear little amazed gasps beside her from Andi and Ash because Celestara knew who she was.

They were invited into the house and Ash and Andi were left to wait with a pile of strange magazines. Sara noticed a large-headed extraterrestrial on the front of one magazine as she was directed into the consultation room.

Celestara lit a candle after they sat at a small table, and invoked an all-inclusive prayer to angels, spirit guides, Jesus, Buddha, Saint Germaine, and all the ET's. Sara was wondering if Celestara was her birth name. It could be, she mused, considering Andi's bohemian parents had named her Andromeda Universe Morrison. The Morrison part was actually her father's last name, not any reference to Jim.

"I sense a lot of anger," Celestara began.

Well no shit, Sara thought. Her lips thinned.

"The Twelve are telling me that you are entering a period of accelerated personal growth and change. The anger is a sign of your resistance."

"The Twelve?"

"My guides are a group of light beings who call themselves The Council of Twelve. If you have any medical questions, I am also in contact with a Doctor Peebles whose last incarnation as a physician was in seventeenth-century Europe."

"Didn't they do bloodletting then?"

Celestara's cosmic gaze wobbled a bit.

"Could you ask your guides why we age?"

Celestara closed her eyes, then, "The Twelve say that you only age because you believe you will. You have to let go of your expectations. Doctor Peebles adds that you have circulatory blockages; he suggests you exercise to move your blocked chi."

"So, am I supposed to accept that I age and exercise to stave it off, or not accept it and eat all the donuts I want?"

"There is no 'supposed to.' You are in charge of your own reality. Hmmm . . ."

Sara sat forward. Celestara was apparently receiving something interesting.

"Yes . . . yes . . . " Celestara was nodding with her eyes closed. Sara fidgeted impatiently until Celestara opened her eyes and continued, "I see a past life in Iceland."

I knew it, Sara thought, that's where I got these Nordic, cottage cheese-filled thighs from. My name was probably Fat Helga.

"You were a married woman, and your husband was a Viking gone at sea most of the time." Celestara closed her eyes again to consult the beyond. "You were young and not inclined to wait for his return. I see many affairs with men of your village."

Sara cringed. Why couldn't she have been Cleopatra, or Joan of

Arc or someone admirable? Why did she have to be a Viking slut with cottage cheese thighs?

"Your husband was killed . . . in a raid . . . it looks like an English coastal village. You cared for your husband and felt guilty for cheating on him . . . yes, very guilty. This is why you sabotage your relationships now. You feel you don't deserve to be loved. You have been doing this in many lifetimes since."

"I don't sabotage my relationships," Sara said at the same time she was thinking that relationship failure always did seem a bit familiar. She scared herself by asking a question she was not sure she wanted the answer to.

"Well, will I ever meet my soulmate and have a lasting relationship?"

Celestara closed her eyes again. She nodded. She listened some more. She nodded. Sara felt sweat forming in her armpits.

The Plan is born

"**S**o what did she say?" Andi asked the minute they were out the door.

"Tell us everything darling," Ash added.

"I was an adulteress in a past life, I actually do have a soulmate, and I now know why my thighs are fat."

"Your thighs aren't fat," Andi said, rolling her eyes to heaven.

"A soulmate," Ash said. "Does that mean one sexual partner for all eternity once you hook up?"

"I would love to find my soulmate!" Andi gushed. "Who is it?"

"I don't know or if I'll ever know. Celestara says he's not what I'm expecting, and if I don't change, he won't show up."

"Darling, we love you just the way you are, fat thighs and all."

"Thanks a lot, Ash."

"How did she say you have to change," asked Andi.

"Something about loving myself."

"Ah," said Andi sagely.

"Tough one," Ash admitted, ruffling his already ruffled hair. "I still hate myself for mean things I did to my brother when I was twelve."

"I love myself," Andi said, a bit guiltily Sara thought.

"You do not," Sara told her. "If you did, why would you hang out with me, a bona fide self-hater?"

"What the bloody hell is wrong with you today?" Ash asked Sara.

"Birthday blues, I told you already," she said.

"No such thing love. It's a contradiction in terms."

"Not if you're over thirty."

Andi brought them back to the issue at hand. "What's not to love about you Sara?"

"Fat deposits, frizzy hair, sucky job, past my prime, shall I go on?"

The whole idea of meeting a soulmate and all of its implications hit Sara suddenly.

"The thighs have got to go! And . . . I need Botox! Look at these crow's feet!" Sara pointed desperately at her hideous eyes.

"Try not smiling," Ash suggested. "They don't show up as badly then."

Sara gaped at Ash with a dropped jaw.

"You don't want to smile just with your lips like some Stepford wife do you?" Andi said.

"All the movie stars do it," Sara pointed out.

"Botox is botulism darling," Ash said. "Do you really want to stick your face with it?"

Just then, a Porsche rumbled by. A fat, gray-haired man with no chin was driving, and a tanned, blonde beauty was sitting next to him. What the hell!

"Yes, I do want Botox. And I want liposuction. I don't want to be left behind with the dregs of the unenhanced. It'll be my birthday present to myself."

As they were driving back to the coffee shop, Sara made plans to become the woman she wanted to be. If she was going to love herself, one thing was sure, she had to stop hating herself.

PART II
The Plan gains momentum

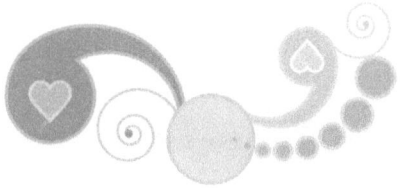

Fun with tarot cards

"I've made my first appointment."

"For what?"

"My beautification process," Sara told Andi.

"Well then, let's start the process of manifesting your soulmate."

"How?"

"Let's see what the tarot cards say."

Andi retrieved a deck and started shuffling. She and Sara were sitting at Andi's kitchen table drinking tea.

"Think about your man."

Sara tried not to think about her hot pink dildo.

"Okay, pick one. No, pick four."

"Don't you know how to do this?"

"Not really. This is just for fun. Lay them down side by side. Oh my stars. That is so weird."

"What?" Sara asked her anxiously. "Am I going to die?"

"You chose all major arcana."

"Major what?"

"They're like the royalty cards in a regular deck. You know, the jack through ace instead of the numbered cards."

"Yeah, but what does that mean?"

"Um . . . don't know."

Andi was flipping through a little booklet intensely while Sara sipped tea. "Wow," she exclaimed, "The Sun means fortunate marriage!"

"Yeah, but what's that one, The Tower—people falling out of a burning building with lightning and explosions? And that one says, The Hanged Man."

Andi ignored this and stated that The High Priestess was Sara. "It's upside-down though, so I don't think you know you're The High Priestess yet." Andi consulted the tiny book. "Actually, it means passion."

Sara rolled her eyes.

"The Hanged Man means wisdom, circumspection, discernment, trials, sacrifice—"

"Jeez," cried Sara. "That doesn't make sense."

"The Tower means . . . well, forget what The Tower means. Sara, I think what the cards are trying to tell you is that you will be going through some changes. Maybe difficult changes . . . "

Both of them glanced uneasily at The Tower.

"I can't read these things anyway," said Andi. "Let's get on the Internet instead."

"What for?"

"You need to put yourself out there. You haven't had a date since Greg."

"I haven't wanted one," Sara lied.

"Okay, you need a profile," Andi said while typing.

"I don't want to do this. Why don't you do it instead," Sara suggested.

"I already do."

"Do I have to put up a photo? If I do, I'll wait until I have plastic surgery."

"Not on all the sites, but would you accept a date without one?" Andi asked.

"Define date. I refuse to stoop to cybersex with spankme2nite."

"No, I'm talking about meeting up with a local. But you can talk to guys around the world. I love just 'chatting.' It's fun. I've got a guy in Holland, one in Nigeria, another in Brazil."

"Sounds exhausting. How about a photo of me when I was twenty-five?"

"You can use a magazine model's photo if you want. No one will know unless you meet in person. If a man says he's not that tall with a few extra pounds for example, you can pretty much figure he looks like Yoda."

"Why am I doing this?"

"Don't you want to find your soulmate?"

"Yeah, but I don't love myself yet so why bother?"

"How about we just check out some guys? What age do you want?"

"Good question," said Sara. "I want him old enough to be financially stable, but young enough to be sexually stable. How's that?"

"Okay. Thirty-five."

"But that's younger than me," Sara pointed out.

"So? Hans is twenty-two."

"Hans?"

"My guy in Holland."

Sara stared at the computer screen and columns of photos and profiles appeared. It was as if she were caught peeing behind a bush or suddenly naked in a mall. She reminded herself that none of these guys knew she was looking at them.

"Adrian. He's kinda cute," said Andi.

"Yeah, but look at that comb-over. Why doesn't he just shave his head and be done with it?"

"How about Doug? He says, 'Laugh for no reason and enjoy life.'"

"Too cheerful, possibly even psychotic. Picture him laughing maniacally at nothing."

"This guy is kinda dark. 'Out on the edge. No mainstreamers. Looking for an open-minded freethinker.'"

"Sounds like we might be talking about a very weird sexual deviant."

"Well," said Andi, "you wanted someone sexually active."

"Stable, I said stable. I want someone who can get it up, not flog me with it."

"Okay, what kind of guy do you want? Describe him."

"Hmmmm," Sara mused. "Independent, creative. I like nice eyes. And smart. He's got to have a three-digit IQ."

"Sounds kinda like Ash. Let's write up a profile for you, and see if we can entice a smart, entrepreneurial Johnny Depp to respond."

"I don't know what to say about myself."

"Think about it. You're a writer. You ought to be able to come up with something."

"You'd think," admitted Sara.

"I've got an idea. Take The High Priestess card with you and maybe you'll get inspired."

Job hell

S ara stared at her computer screen, where she was supposed to be writing ad copy for a Mexican restaurant. Ad copy was excruciatingly boring. She wanted to write intense espionage novels, or maybe a new diet book that would make her thin and rich at the same time.

She took a sip of "awffee." Awffee was Sara's name for office coffee, which of course was always awful. But she indulged anyway, since nasty-tasting caffeine and sugar to get through the day was better than no drugs at all.

She glanced at The High Priestess card, which she had stuck to her corkboard.

She began typing: "Gorgeous, tanned Ph.D. looking for rich, virile Johnny Depp look-alike."

"Sara."

Sara looked up at her boss, Kyle, creative director for T-Squared.

"Hey Kyle."

Kyle's eyes strayed to Sara's screen. Sara felt the skin tightening on her scalp.

"What's up?" she asked to grab his eyes. Then fiddled with the general disarray on her desk to further distract him.

Kyle smiled flashing his whitened teeth.

Sara made a mental note to add teeth-whitening to her Plan.

Kyle was the owners' son. He was tall, good-looking, and full of himself. Why did she have to work for someone younger than herself? There was something very wrong about that. If he was bad at his job she could have really worked up a case against him.

"Would you mind sitting in on a meeting for me and taking notes?" Kyle asked, glancing at his watch.

"Where's Karen?" Sara was thinking that his own assistant might be a better choice for secretarial duties than his copywriter who was currently very busy writing copy for a restaurant ad.

"Out sick. Shouldn't take too long. Just an intro on a new client."

"Okay," Sara agreed while wondering why Kyle was blowing off the meeting. Sounded pretty important to her. Being the owners' son, Sara figured he probably had to get his nails buffed or something.

When Sara entered the conference room, Mr. T was seated at the head of the table like God in an Armani suit. The account exec who'd landed the account was preening himself. Various team members were tapping on smart screens importantly or opening laptops. Sara seated herself with a pad of paper and a ballpoint pen. Mrs. T sailed in last, looking chic and well maintained for her sixty-plus years. Sara would have loved to ask Mrs. T what work she'd had done and how much it had cost.

Mr. T instructed the account exec, Matt, to fill everyone in on the client.

"Young At Heart, LLC produces personal care products for the elderly."

Oh no, Sara thought, adult diapers.

"So far, they have limited their selling to pharmacies and direct snail-mail. They want an updated look for their products and an expanded Internet presence. Older folks are getting computer savvy."

"We want to suggest other venues as well. I want to see an upbeat approach on the product look," Mr. T said. "Let's make it fun."

Fun, Sara wrote on her pad, adding some fleur-de-lis.

"Right. The baby boomers are all getting old, and they like to have fun. Remember the sixties," Mrs. T added, while silently commanding the room to forget that she was in fact a baby boomer herself.

"What personal care products are we talking about?" asked a cheerful but very serious team member.

After a short pause Matt said, "Incontinence products," with a straight face. He then put on a pair of glasses and read from a list, "protective underwear, liners, underpads, belted and beltless undergarments. They also carry a plus-size product line."

Sara saw Matt bite his bottom lip trying not to smile. She felt the entire room of T-Squared employees wondering how old Mr. T was, and what might be lurking under the Armani suit.

To hide her speculation about Mr. T, Sara drew a stick figure and added a diaper. Then made a note for her Plan: "Work out groin muscles to stave off incontinence."

"We could add flower prints to the underpants, make them pretty. Or, say, stripes to a men's line."

"How about neon colors?"

"A thong version."

There was subdued laughter at that one.

"How about a "green" version made from recycled materials?"

"The baby boomers would love that."

"TV ads. We'll make it look trendy."

"Like Viagra and depression medication."

Sara no longer wondered why Kyle had skipped out on this meeting. She added stripes to her stick figure's diaper.

"Radio too. A granny going out dancing. Rock music from the sixties."

"Grandpa rock climbing with the right protective gear."

"Good, good," Mr. T said. "We've got two weeks to come up with a presentation."

Sara stopped in the ladies room on the way back to her desk. She felt the urge to empty her bladder.

What she saw in there stopped her in her tracks. One of the new graphic designers—an extremely pierced girl whose stick-straight hair was a lovely shade of purple—and Jan from accounts payable were in a liplock worthy of a porn flick.

They didn't even notice Sara. She peed, washed her hands, hummed a few bars of *Frère Jacques* and headed to the break room for more awffee.

She passed two team members talking passionately about incontinence pads printed with the American flag.

Angelica, the receptionist, was making coffee. Sara watched Angelica carefully measure the correct amount of grounds counting each scoop out loud. She stayed for the agonizingly slow ritual of replacing the lid on the coffee can while trying not to scream. Then she left before Angelica could begin the process of putting the can away without breaking her nails.

On the way back to her desk Sara glared at Brittney, who was dressed to the nines as usual and talking to Mr. T cheerfully as he tried not to stare at her cleavage.

Back at her computer Sara started typing, Depressed female seeks messianic savior to deliver her from the corporate evil of the world.

An email came in from Andi. She said she'd rather drink boiling bleach than design flower prints for adult diapers.

Mrs. T peaked over the wall of Sara's cubicle. Mrs. T could never quite suppress a look of slight distaste at the untidiness of Sara's workstation. However, used to creative types as she was, Mrs. T ignored it without actually appearing to do so.

"Hey Mrs. T, what's up?" said Sara, while minimizing the window displaying her progress on the Mexican restaurant ad.

"Zebra Productions has its office opening tonight. Kyle suggested you go and do a little write-up on the affair."

"Well, actually . . ." Sara was thinking furiously of the reason she couldn't do this, while at the same time, wondering why Kyle always wanted her to do everything.

"Congressman Bank is supposed to be there. Thanks Sara. Six-thirty. Don't forget."

Mrs. T smiled at Sara with her lips only.

The snag

On the long list of things Sara did not like, having to attend an office opening was somewhere near the top.

In the first place, Sara had to fish through her closet for something to wear around all the glitzy guests trying to outglitz each other. This wouldn't have been so irritating if her thighs weren't so full of cottage cheese.

There was only one outfit up to the task—a black, spaghetti-strap cocktail dress with a flared hemline, which drew attention away from the cottage cheese.

Her hair was another story. It had a mind of its own, and it was in a frizzy mood. She peered at the roots. There was a half-inch of mousy brown glaringly speckled with ugly grays before the auburn started.

*

Aaaargh!

*

After an hour of curling, flattening and spraying to achieve the magical combination that would suddenly make her look fabulous, Sara gave up and put on more makeup. More mascara made clumps in her eyelashes. She was about to wash it off and redo it, when she looked at the time.

Great, she was already late.

On the way out the door she snagged her nylons.

In the ladies restroom at Zebra Productions, Sara sat on the toilet in a stall and applied clear nail polish to the snag in her nylons. She always kept a bottle in her purse for such emergencies.

"Where did you get your boobs done?" asked some girl at the sinks.

"Doctor Lo. I got these and landed the Sport's Pro commercials. Dr. Lo's this itty-bitty Asian guy who specializes in breast augmentation. You should check him out."

"Yeah, I'm thinking about having some fat sucked out first."

Sara emerged from the stall and looked at the two anorexic, barely adult actresses. She knew they were actresses because everyone had a nametag with their job identities stuck to them somewhere.

You've got to be kidding, Sara thought as she took in the stick figures before her, the fat that girl was referring to must be in her brain.

The two actresses smiled at Sara with their lips while their eyes assessed her as competition, dismissed her, then smiled at her with their whole faces.

Sara washed her hands and tried not to look at her clumpy eyelashes and frizzy hair in the mirror.

Back out in the party, Sara scanned the room for Congressman Bank. He wasn't there. After a little inquiry, she found out he had sent his assistant in his stead.

The assistant, Janet Norbit, was talking to a small group of panting sycophants about the coming election and why Congressman Bank was running again. The sycophants offered little snippets for video they could shoot to promote his platform.

Sara got out her tiny notebook. She was old-fashioned and resisted modern technology. On the other hand, she could not imagine trying to write with a typewriter. It occurred to her that she wasn't really old-fashioned at all. She was just contrary.

So be it, she thought. Part of loving myself would be to embrace my bad qualities, right?

"You look fabulous."

Sara glanced up at Kyle, looking sleek in a glitzy Italian suit. His golden hair and tanned complexion spelled vacation in Cancun, rich, relaxed. She backed away from him slightly so he wouldn't see the clumps in her eyelashes.

"Bank didn't show," she said by way of ignoring his compliment which she knew was a platitude.

"No, but look. There's Ever Vessence."

Sara followed Kyle's eyes to a sparkling, augmented, platinum-haired beauty. "Who's that?" she asked.

Kyle smirked. "She's a model. A rather famous one."

Sara looked at Kyle and thought she saw him salivating.

He tore his eyes away from Ever and looked at Sara. "Advertising is changing fast. No one looks much at print anymore. Internet is the way to go. Magazines, newspapers, they're all online."

Sara couldn't see the segue between Ever and the Internet. Then again, she probably could.

"Yeah, it's easier to shop online, read online," Sara admitted. "It's usually free and you can do it in the nude."

Kyle looked at Sara and she recalled a terrifying dream she'd had of finding herself nude in a public place and not knowing how to get out unseen.

"Well, you can read magazines and newspapers in the nude too, but you can't link to other related sites. And TV is watered down. Satellite and cable have a zillion stations between them."

"At least a zillion," Sara added while wondering why Kyle was going on about this when so many luscious morsels like Ever were just waiting to be plucked by young, successful creative directors.

"You're making fun of me."

Sara backpedaled. "Oh no, I'm laughing with you."

"But I'm not laughing." Kyle looked miffed. Or did he look hurt?

At this point, while resisting an inexplicable urge to laugh hysterically at or with Kyle, Sara noticed a young, artist-type wielding a video camera while duck-walking very near her.

That urge evaporated however, when she saw her snagged, nail-polished nylon stretched over her cottage cheese thigh displayed on the wall monitors.

"Do you want to get a drink?" she asked Kyle while moving out of camera range and pulling her dress down.

"Maybe later," Kyle said, smiling again. "I've got some business to do while here. But I want to follow up on this conversation . . . later."

"Later," Sara said, wondering if this was yet another task Kyle wanted to pile on her already overflowing plate. When was she ever going to find time to write a profile? It was typical of employers to heap more work on you without any additional monetary compensation.

Sara saw Kyle talking to Ever and handing her a glass of champagne. Yeah right, she thought, I get menial tasks and Ever gets champagne.

Instead of making notes on the office opening, Sara worked on her to-do list.

1. Facial
2. Liposuction
3. Botox
4. Whiten teeth
5. Stray pubic hair removal
6. Lip injections
7. ~~Breast augmentation~~
8. Crow's feet surgery
9. Work out

Sara crossed out breast augmentation. Every month her breasts were so sore from PMS, she could not face surgical recovery for that area.

That done, she drifted to the food table to note its splendor for the write-up.

"And what do you think of Zebra Productions new premises . . ."

Sara spun around into the camera held by the duck-walker. She saw her face huge in the wall monitors out of the corner of her eye.

". . . Sara from T-Squared?"

"I think they're—" Sara dropped the hors d'oeuvre she was holding and bent down to pick it up so the camera would stop filming her flaws. She felt the snag give way and her nylons run. As she came up, she saw her butt, her cottage cheese thigh and the run in her black nylons in the monitor.

"Piss off," she said to the camera.

The room got quieter and Sara noticed the cameraman had in fact not pissed off. If anything, he was looking as though he'd hit the jackpot.

She reached over and stuck the hors d'oeuvre, which was a carrot stick with cream cheese and a mint leaf, through the half-inch gage stretching his left earlobe.

Then, she left the party before things could get any worse.

Refuge in the bookstore

Sara entered Bookaholic, Ash's second-hand bookstore, and was relieved to find Ash still there.

"Where's Maddy?" Sara asked him. Maddy was Ash's one long-suffering employee, who did everything from the accounting to cleaning the bathroom.

"Gone home, love. She's sick of the sight of me."

"Good." Sara wanted to talk to Ash alone. Besides, Maddy was nice and all, but she slunk silently around the bookstore like a vampire, and her pasty complexion and black hair added to the effect.

Ash looked up from the book he was mending. "You look fabulous darling. Are you going out on a date?"

"Do you have some rum? Painkillers? Any drug will do."

Ash pulled a pint of Jack Daniels from his desk drawer. "Knock yourself out," he told Sara.

Sara slammed down a swig and coughed. "I hate my job. I hate my thighs. My boyfriend is a dildo—"

"You don't have a boyfriend." Then Ash got it and added, "Oh."

Sara continued, "I just made a spectacular fool of myself, and it's on film."

"Bloody hell. What did you do on film?"

Two goggle-eyed elderly ladies in the religious section were staring over at them and whispering to each other.

"Oh, nothing. I was just at an office opening. Hateful."

"Hateful," parroted Ash.

"What would you know about it? You don't have to do anything. I wish my parents were rich and could buy me a cushy little business."

"Hey, I work hard around here."

"I know. You're a workaholic at Bookaholic. But still . . ."

"What kind of business would you want?"

"Something where I could be creative. I just can't work up any passion over adult diaper ads."

"Are we avoiding the real issue here? Your lack of a sex life?"

Sara collapsed on Ash's messy desktop and cried.

The elderly ladies moved a bit closer.

"I told you," Sara finally said sniffling, "I have a sex life. It just doesn't include a sentient partner."

Ash offered Sara the bottle. She took another swig.

"I'm supposed to be writing a profile. Andi thinks Internet dating might help me find my soulmate."

"If nothing else, it's a step up from masturbation."

The elderly ladies left Bookaholic in a huff.

"Oops," said Sara, "I didn't know those ladies were here."

"Don't worry about them. They are the Misses Wilson, Ethel and Hazel. They come here for this sort of thing. They love it. It'll give them something to be outraged at. Now," said Ash as he opened his laptop, "let's write your profile."

Sara dried her eyes on a tissue. Clumps of mascara came off.

Ash looked at Sara's raccoon eyes, then began, "Gorgeous, creative female, looking—"

"I'm not gorgeous."

"Attractive, creative, thirty-something female, looking for soulmate—"

"That's too obvious. Let me see . . . Do you think I'm attractive Ash? Tell the truth."

Ash did think Sara was attractive, but felt as though this was somehow a trick question. So when he answered yes, he looked guilty.

"You think I'm fat and old don't you? Admit it!" Sara grabbed the Jack and took another pull.

"Sara, shut up. You look sensational. I happen to like fat thighs and raccoon eyes. We British blokes aren't as picky as American men. Hardly anybody has good teeth back home for instance."

After a shocked pause, Sara laughed and looked into Ash's crazy brown eyes, which were somewhat obscured by his rakish hairstyle.

"Okay. I'll put up a photo, so I don't have to say anything about the way I look—they can decide for themselves. Headline should read . . . Looking for someone different. Then: If your idea of fun is watching sports on TV, don't bother me."

"Ooh, harsh."

Sara's creative juices were flowing now, thanks in some measure to the Jack. "High priestess looking for a Renaissance man to have great conversations with. Nice eyes a plus. Three-digit IQ mandatory."

"Sounds confrontational." Ash observed. "Did you have a past life in Egypt as a high priestess too, aside from the Viking gig?"

"No. It's a tarot card that Andi said represented me. I'm not going to really date anybody anyway, so who cares what I say?"

"Not I," Ash said.

"Hey, wait a minute. I don't have to answer anybody who contacts me, right?"

"No. You don't have to do anything darling—it's your life . . . and your personal ad. Let's post this on the site I'm on for starters—it's local."

Sara yawned. "I've got to get home."

"It's Friday night. Will you turn into a pumpkin if you stay?"

"The carriage turns into a pumpkin Ash. The princess—that's me—turns back into a poor slaving copywriter. But not until Monday. I have an early appointment with an aesthetician tomorrow."

"What the bloody hell is that?"

"I'm having my face sanded."

PART III
The fun begins

Sara learns that pain is the path to beauty

U p until the point that Sara's face began to burn like hellfire things were peachy.

The consultation was encouraging. Skintastic could wipe years off Sara's face with no downtime. They could melt fat and eliminate unwanted hair with lasers. They even had strings they implanted to pull saggy faces up.

Which seemed a plausible alternative to carving up the face and stitching it back together in a traditional facelift.

Sara enjoyed having her face washed and dried. The aesthetician, whose name was Janelle, explained that she was going to apply a chemical peel first before the microdermabrasion. She tailored the peel to Sara's skin type and it would consist of three layers.

When she handed Sara a minifan, Sara wondered why.

The first layer tingled a little. By the time the third layer got brushed on, Sara almost jumped off the table. She thought the layer must be battery acid.

"Okay?" asked Janelle. "Five more minutes."

Sara said she was okay through clenched teeth even though it felt as though millions of Lilliputians were viciously stabbing her face with needles.

Relief was immediate as soon as the chemicals were rinsed off. Sara sagged on the table. She was exhausted.

Then Janelle started the microderm. It was a little rotating diamond head that "sanded" off the dead skin cells and sucked them up like a vacuum cleaner.

Sara's whole face felt like dead skin after the battery acid layer.

Janelle sanded and sucked every inch of Sara's traumatized face. But Sara found herself noticing little spots Janelle missed and worrying that it was being done in a nonsymmetrical way. It was exactly like being back in grade school when the teacher would erase the chalkboard, and Sara would be sitting at her desk in agony because the teacher missed spots of chalk.

She recalled the tension in her little eight-year-old body—which by the way was totally free of cottage cheese—silently willing the teacher with every ounce of her being to please get all the chalk off.

*

Aaaargh!

*

Sara was ready for counseling when it was all over. She had discovered in herself hitherto unknown depths of OCD and masochism.

Nevertheless, on her way out she made an appointment for Botox and lip injections. She was determined to see her Plan out.

Back at the bookstore

"**Y**ou look like a shiny apple. That's good, right?"

"Ash, don't be mean," said Andi. "Your face isn't that red Sara. It's pink. It is shiny though. But that IS good, right?"

"Right," said Sara, "just peachy."

"Not peachy love. There is no peach fuzz left. They sanded it all off. Or burned it off as the case may be."

"Not all of it. The teacher always misses spots of chalk with that damn eraser."

Ash and Andi looked at each other. Sara wasn't one bit closer to loving herself.

"I know," said Ash. "Let's check your inbox for interested men."

This idea shocked Sara out of her post-facial depression. Her heart started beating in her throat.

"By the way Sara, Hans says hi."

"Who's Hans?" Ash asked.

"Just a guy in Holland I talk to. I told him about Sara. Sara, he's got some friends who would like to hook up with you."

Sara said she didn't want a long-distance relationship, especially one that involved a webcam. She wanted the privilege of looking like hell in the privacy of her own home.

Ash: "No, can't be real."

Andi: "Oh my stars, will you look at him."

Ash: "Must be a fake photo."

Andi: "He's a definite ten."

"What!" cried Sara. "What are you going on about?"

Ash swiveled the laptop around. "Check it out."

"If you don't want to meet him," said Andi, "I will."

"I'll definitely have to get my roots dyed first," Sara said.

Kyle

S ara watched as Brittney strutted by wearing a suit that must have cost her a month's pay. Her hair was perfectly coiffed and she looked as though she'd stopped at Neiman Marcus on the way to work to have her makeup done.

What a butt-kisser, Sara thought. She was grateful she had a job that did not require her to dress up. She liked wearing clothes she could slouch in.

Brittney strutted back across the room, tap tap tapping her heels importantly. Sara stuck her finger in her mouth and pretended to gag.

Eventually, Brittney tapped over to Sara's desk and handed her a flash drive. "Sara, here's the copy Future Signs gave us for their brochure. I'm sure you can do better than them. You're skin's peeling you know."

Sara stared at Brittney with radioactive loathing. "Yeah, I know," she said in a dangerous monotone.

"I'm taking over the account," Brittney added. "Can you have the copy for me tomorrow?"

"But you're just a designer," Sara pointed out.

Brittney filled Sara in on Mr. T's decision to give her more responsibilities ad nauseam. Such close proximity made it impossible for Sara to ignore the rock on Brittney's ring finger, which she had been doing successfully up until now. Well, Greg did have a cushy, high-paid, boring accounting job. Thank goodness Greg worked on another floor and she never had to see HIM.

"Hey Britt. Ready for lunch? Oh, hi Sara. Haven't seen you in ages."

Sara looked up at Greg, who had just walked up behind Brittney and was massaging her shoulder.

"What's wrong with your face?" he asked.

"Nothing."

Sara went back to writing the script for Young At Heart, LLC's thirty-second spot on cable. She glued her eyes to the screen until the happy couple departed. May they both rot in hell.

An email came in from Mrs. T. She wanted to see Sara in her office. Sara gladly left the adult diaper gig and headed out.

"What's wrong with your face?" asked Mrs. T as soon as Sara walked in.

"Facial," Sara told her.

Mrs. T nodded with comprehension.

"Sara, we had to bring a few of the newsletters we were farming out in-house. Kyle said you could handle them. It would be easier for you to just go ahead and lay them out yourself, rather than use one of the designers."

"But, the Young At Heart—"

"Is looking great. Love the retired couple rollerblading bit." She handed Sara an interdepartmental envelope and uttered a firm, Thank you.

Sara slunk out of Mrs. T's office. She was beginning to see the picture now. Kyle was trying to get her to quit by piling her up with too much work and no more money. He wanted to hire some young, IQ-challenged, platinum-haired chick he could wrap around his manicured little finger and have sex with in his office.

Back at her desk Andi showed up. "Aren't you seeing Mr. Gorgeous tonight?" she said excitedly.

This reminder sent Sara into paroxysms of terror.

"Yeah, we're meeting for awffee, I mean coffee. What can I do about my peeling skin? I'm flaking like piecrust from that facial. And I itch."

"Tell your date you just came back from The Bahamas. Wanna go to lunch?"

Kyle walked up. Sara's lips thinned. "Too busy with EXTRA work," she told Andi. "I might have time to eat in a month or two. You go. I'll just chew some cud."

"Hey Sara," Kyle said. "Got a minute?"

Sara stared at Kyle. Didn't he hear that bit about not having enough time to eat?

"Sure," she told him. Why not just sign up now for the one-woman ad agency show and be done with it?

"You know the other night at—what's wrong with your face?"

"Nothing," she told him while scratching her chin. A shower of white skin flakes rained down on her desk.

"Minipeel, right?"

"Well, okay, yes."

"I wanted to run a few things by you. How about a liquid lunch?" Kyle held up two bottles of Greens Galore Protein-Packed Smoothie.

So that's how Kyle stays so thin and fit thought Sara as he pulled up a chair without waiting for her answer.

"Most marketing plays it safe."

Sara wasn't sure how to respond to this, so she nodded.

"They stick to the tried and true. But the tech world is changing fast. Consumers are getting younger and younger."

"That's truc," Sara admitted. "When I was twelve, I didn't have a credit card."

"You're funny," Kyle said. Was Kyle making fun of her? "Attention spans have been squeezed," he continued. "The tech-savvy, short-attention span, immediate gratification market is not being exploited as it could be."

"What do you have in mind? A new venue?"

"Yes. Precisely. Picture an Internet video browser entirely devoted to interactive commercials. It's a global market." Kyle's pupils were dilating.

"But, don't most people fast-forward past commercials? Why would they go to a site with just commercials?"

"For information. Commercials that are interactive, game-like. Where you choose answers. Not only that, kids love commercials. And the caveat here is that the ads would be really creative, out of the box creative. That's where you come in."

"Me?"

"You're the most creative person on this staff."

Sara suspected Kyle was buttering her up for nonstop overtime developing his pet project.

"Think about it. The future of this country as I see it is entrepreneurial. We can't compete with overseas manufacturing. We will become a nation of business owners—many of them Internet and the service industries to support them. They all need global advertising."

Sara chewed on this idea.

"For now," Kyle told her, "keep this under your hat."

He downed his drink and left with a wink. Sara sat scratching her itching chin wondering what she was going to do with another project heaped on her already overflowing workload.

On the other hand, it was an exciting prospect—new territory instead of boring newspaper ads and one-line billboards. On the way out of the office that night she saw Kyle.

"I'm in," she told him.

He smiled. And for the first time, Sara noticed that Kyle had a really nice smile.

The date

S ara arrived at The Coffee Blast sweating. She had no idea how Ash and Andi had talked her into this. At the moment, her brain didn't seem to be functioning at all. She was operating solely from a glandular fight-or-flight response.

Her heart leapt out of her chest when she spotted Mr. Gorgeous.

She was about to turn and run out when he saw her. He sprang up from the table he had secured and walked to her smiling. Sara's knees turned to water.

"Sara?" he said, extending a tanned hand. "I'm Todd. Nice to meet you."

"You too," Sara managed to say without stuttering. Her face itched horribly but there was no way she was going to scratch it.

"What would you like?"

Sara found a table while Todd got her a latte. Ordinarily, she would have insisted upon buying her own, but she didn't seem capable of coherent thought. She did however have a lucid moment imagining the berating she was going to give Ash and Andi.

Todd came back with drinks for them both. Sara tried not to stare at him, but he was even more handsome in person.

Sara thanked him and took the latte.

"Your wish is my command," Todd said smiling.

A few seconds ticked by. Todd seemed to be waiting for Sara to speak first.

Out of desperation to break the silence, Sara asked, "So what do you do?"

"For work? I have a gallery."

"An art gallery? Where?"

"Downtown. It's in an old neighborhood—a 1940's cottage. I'm online as well, of course."

"How interesting. What kind of art?"

"Photography mostly. I think you'd like it. I do quite well in a certain market."

Sara thought he'd put a strange emphasis on "certain." Or maybe he was looking at her oddly because he'd noticed the flakes on her face.

"I just got back from The Bahamas." Sara waved a finger toward her chin. "Peeling you know."

"Oh. Sounds nice. I've never been to the Bahamas. And what do you do?"

"I'm a writer."

"Wow, perfect."

"Perfect for what?"

"Some joint ventures perhaps," Todd said cryptically. "I take it you don't like Sunday football."

"No," admitted Sara. "And you? I take it you don't either, I mean, you answered my ad."

"I'll like anything you want me to like."

Sara was taken aback. What the hell did that mean?

"I respect women. In fact, I consider myself the Renaissance man you asked for. Not a vanilla bone in my body."

"Vanilla?" Sara said.

"What flavor do you prefer?"

"Well, I used to like strawberry, but now chocolate is my favorite," Sara said, thinking that Todd must have an ice cream obsession.

"And I wouldn't want to 'switch,' if you know what I mean."

"Well," Sara said, "it's always good to try new things."

Todd chuckled.

Sara started picking at her chin.

Todd sipped coffee, then said, "So . . . great." Then he lowered his voice in a conspiratorial manner. "I have a collar, or would you prefer to pick one out for me?"

Sara jumped. What the hell? Did he say collar?

"Collar. Did you say collar?"

He nodded and she felt a hand on her knee beneath the table.

"Stop that," Sara told him.

"Okay," Todd said casting his eyes down. "I'll do whatever you want, my priestess. I am your slave. Command me."

"Shit!" Sara gripped the coffee cup so hard the top flew off and coffee splattered. Her hand burned from the coffee and Todd grabbed the cup, and her hand, and tried to suck on her burned fingers.

Sara could finally think coherently again. She commanded Todd to get her some ice and clean up the mess—which he was happy to do—and she left.

Back at the bookstore

"Jeez Andi, he was a sub? What the hell is a sub—I mean, apart from some lettuce and tomato between two buns?"

"Submissive. You know the term, Dominatrix, right?"

"Crap," Sara said. "We've got to edit that posting. But, what does vanilla mean?"

"Vanilla means you like normal . . . sex," Andi told her with pink cheeks.

"Bloody hell," said Ash. "I like normal sex too. Anybody interested?"

Andi's cheeks got pinker.

Maddy silently emerged from sci-fi with a duster. Her black hair, black clothes and stealth made her blend in as a background feature. She'd have been invisible without her pasty complexion. She lifted her chin briefly by way of saying hello, shot a look at Ash then disappeared into the back room.

"And let me guess: a switch can play either side of the equation," Sara mused.

"Right," said Andi.

"Exactly how do you know so much about this?" Ash asked Andi.

Sara was busy wondering what sort of weird sex Maddy was into, and if it happened at the morgue. "Internet dating is insane."

Andi never answered Ash.

"Think of it this way love," Ash prophesied as he typed on his computer, "every failure is one more step toward success."

"I'm not taking any more steps," Sara told him. "I'm going to hire the cabana boys."

Ash turned the laptop toward her. "Yeah?" he said, "take a look at this guy. Says he's a physicist so he must have a three-digit IQ. No photo, but he sounds doable."

"I'm off," said Maddy, emerging from the back room where she had probably been dusting off her coffin. "Unless you need anything else?"

"No, love," Ash told her. "Toodles."

As Maddy quietly left the bookstore, Sara turned her attention back to the doable prospect with no photo. There was always time to hire cabana boys later.

Change is a good thing, right?

Sara wrapped up the copy for Future Signs and sent it to Brittney via email. She had to admit that she actually loved modern technology. How else could you communicate with people and avoid them at the same time?

Andi showed up and handed Sara a latte. "Went to Coffee Blast at break. I needed some serious caffeine, not that colored water Angelica makes."

"You mean the awffee?"

"The awffee. By the way, your skin looks good now that you're not shedding anymore."

"Why are you in need of drugs?" Sara asked, "This is a triple, right?"

"David got a senior designer position. Probably because of his muscle tone. Mrs. T always smiles at him. And of course he smiles back."

"In that case, I'm surprised Brittney didn't get the position for showing Mr. T her cleavage at every possible opportunity. But what about you? Haven't you been here longer than David?"

"Yeah. But I don't have any cleavage or muscle tone. I've been thinking; do you want to try working out at a gym again?"

"Working out doesn't really work out for me." Sara cringed at her own laziness, remembering that she had added "working out" to her Plan.

"Well, I've been seeing someone local. He has good muscle tone." Andi blushed. "Hey, aren't you having another date tonight too? With the physicist?"

"Yeah," Sara admitted. "I'm meeting him at Bookaholic. That way Ash can be my backup in case the guy is another psycho. Are you falling for Mr. Muscle Tone?"

"No," said Andi, "just having fun. I still talk to Hans, Kwaku, Thiago. And Sara, subs aren't psychos. Gotta go."

Sara sipped the latte and got out her notebook. She had jotted some ideas down for Kyle's secret project and was hoping to talk to him. She hadn't seen Mr. or Mrs. T for that matter either. Maybe they were all on a private jet to The Bahamas for lunch.

An email came in from Andi. It said: News flash. Kyle is gone. No one knows why. He just doesn't work here anymore. Thought I'd be the first to tell you and make your day.

Sara read the email three times. She couldn't believe it. Kyle gone? But he was the owners' progeny. He had a firm grip on the silver spoon. Where the hell was he? They were supposed to be working on the secret project together.

It was that time of the month and Sara felt like crying, or killing, she wasn't sure which. She couldn't do either however as she had the date later, and now that her skin had stopped flaking she didn't want to ruin her appearance with swollen red eyes or a striped jail outfit.

She looked at The High Priestess, who was even now glaring back at Sara with disdain.

But why would Kyle get her all worked up over this new project right before he flew the coop?

Whatever, she thought. Might as well get back to writing the dialogue between the two granny's wearing Young At Heart undergarments, who can't decide whether to go skydiving or bungee jumping.

"Sara, hey." It was Greg. What the hell was he doing at her desk again this week after not seeing her for ages?

He was holding out an envelope looking sheepish. For one disjointed moment, Sara thought they were back in their boring relationship and he was giving her a late birthday card as usual.

"I'd love you to come—for old time's sake. To my wedding that is."

Sara took the envelope as though it might be filled with anthrax. "Old time's sake," she said.

"Anyway, see you around."

Sara drew a gingerbread man shape on the envelope with Greg's hairstyle. Then she attached it to her corkboard and stuck pins in it.

She began writing the copy.

Granny One: My husband finally died. My goodness, it's about time. I'm sick of having intercourse when my bladder is so leaky.

Granny Two: I know what you mean dear. But now that I've discovered Young At Heart undergarments, I feel like a new woman.

Granny One: You mean, it makes intercourse more palatable and less messy?

Granny Two: Oh no dear. But the Young At Heart black protective thongs with the printed skulls scare my husband away every time.

Granny One: I wish I'd known about Young At Heart years ago!

Sara finished off the latte and thought about her appointment tomorrow for Botox and lip injections. If her bank account survived the beautification process, then maybe she could love herself and her soulmate would show up.

She checked her account balance online. She had enough for the injections and various minor enhancements, but she had no idea how she was going to pay for liposuction.

Liposuction was The Holy Grail. If the cottage cheese was gone from her thighs, Sara thought she could actually have sex with a sentient partner with the lights on.

Sara saw Mrs. T with Brittney. They were walking toward her. Brittney was smiling cheerfully as usual. Actually, she looked more than cheerful. Mrs. T was probably helping her hand out wedding invitations.

When they arrived at her desk, Sara started to say that she'd already gotten an invite from Greg.

She was stopped short however when Mrs. T made an announcement.

Brittney was the new creative director.

Mrs. T was smiling with her lips only.

PART IV
Things can always get worse

A surprise in store

Sara didn't give a remote rat's ass what she looked like for the date. She was too pissed about Brittney.

Brittney . . . the slut!

Pissed was, of course, an understatement of epic proportions.

This at least took the edge off her nervousness. If her date was a freak, Sara didn't need Ash's protection. She'd beat the shit out of him herself.

The minute she was in Bookaholic, instead of pretending to be a customer, Sara spilled the whole story to Ash, who, being British, took it calmly.

"The bitch! The bloody bitch! Brittney is so dead."

Sara agreed, but murder was tricky.

"Isn't there a way to slip her some poison, or arrange a fatal accident?" she asked the ceiling.

"I know love, we could irritate her to death by gatecrashing her wedding."

"Won't work. I'm invited," Sara told him.

"No way."

"Way."

Ash was pondering this absurdity when a young man walked up to pay for a book. Ash reached for the book but the young man said, "No. It's for the lady."

Sara looked up into the eyes of her date. He was cute, but she wasn't sure he was entirely out of puberty yet. He looked older in the photo he'd sent her. How could he have a master's degree in physics?

"I overheard your conversation. Sorry for eavesdropping. I wanted to check you out first so I browsed in spirituality."

The young man shrugged and grinned.

"Bloody hell," said Ash, while Sara continued to gape.

She just could not work up any anger at him though. He was cute *and* honest.

"Sara, I'm Bryan," he said extending his hand.

Sara took it. "This is my friend Ash. This is his bookstore."

"Awesome," said Bryan as he shook hands with Ash and pulled up a chair.

"What's the book?" Sara asked, feeling like a mother speaking to her amiable teen.

"Well Sara, it's a book of spells. Why not put a little hoax on your enemy? Bring her a little bad luck. No need to kill her." He was grinning again.

Ash burst out laughing. "Brilliant. Let's make a voodoo doll right now. There's an antique shop next door. I'm sure they have a mangy old Barbie we can use."

"No, not voodoo. This book is more like a set of rituals that use intention, or focus."

"Scientists aren't usually into this sort of thing, being empirical and all," Sara pointed out. "I thought you had a masters in physics."

"I do. Did you know that in the subatomic world if something is observed, it changes into something else? I am a scientist, but I also like to think I'm an explorer."

"So what exactly do you explore?" Ash said, with a mischievous jigging of his eyebrows.

Sara was now wishing she had not picked Bookaholic for the rendezvous.

"Don't mind Ash," Sara told Bryan. "He's British."

"What does that mean?" Ash said. To Bryan he said, "Sara's main descriptor is 'sarcastic.'"

"No, I would call Sara witty," said Bryan.

"Thank you," Sara said. She was warming up to Bryan and wondering how old he really was.

Ash got called away for help with a customer in the romance section.

"How old are you," Sara asked Bryan. "Your age said thirty-five."

"Old enough."

Sara narrowed her eyes.

"Twenty-six," Bryan told her, leaning forward in his chair. "I like older women. Not the kind who like 'boys.' So I lie about my age."

Twenty-six, thought Sara, that's not too bad.

But thirteen years did sound like a pretty big gap, not to mention very unlucky.

On the other hand, she'd never heard of a twenty-six-year-old who couldn't get it up.

Sex with a sentient partner

Bryan dimmed the lights and selected an Internet radio station with ambient music. His apartment was very austere, Sara thought, but clean.

He came up behind her and rubbed her shoulders. "You've got rocks in there," he said.

"Bad day at work," Sara told him, "as you heard while eavesdropping in the spirituality section."

Bryan's smirking lips were on her neck. Sara was so ready for this —particularly now that the lights were dimmed.

She had already done the whole should-I-have-sex-on-the-first-date routine while driving to his apartment, and thrown out all the arguments against it.

Screw conversation, getting to know each other, and moral considerations.

Bryan ran his hands lightly over her breasts. She swung around and they kissed. Bryan's tongue was pierced. His kisses were intense and deliciously wanton.

Sara scored him a nine-point-five. Then she forgot about scores and ratings.

He guided her to the sofa and they began casting off clothes furiously. Bryan's body was lean but fit. And there was no mistaking the rock-solid proof that Bryan wanted her.

Sara's obsession with her cottage cheese thighs completely slipped her mind. Bryan had her pressed against the arm of the sofa. Her lips were locked on his, tongues mingling deliciously.

Hot.

Steamy.

He slipped inside her after putting on a condom so fast it was a blur. After pausing to savor the moment of that first plunge, he pounded into her and she pounded back, both of them responding with vocals likely heard by neighboring apartment dwellers.

It had been a long time, for Sara anyway.

Sara was reminded that while dildos did exactly what you wanted them to do, sex with a sentient partner was much more exciting.

After a very respectable length of time, and many more moans and whisperings, Bryan collapsed and panted, "That was fantastic."

"I hope the walls aren't too thin," Sara managed to gasp out.

Bryan laughed. Then he kissed her, creating a wave of heat that re-stoked the fires.

"Let's do it again," he said. "Slower this time."

Injections

Sara sat in the treatment chair at Skintastic reliving sex with Bryan. They had done it three times and she could barely walk at work the next day. He had actually cooked her dinner between the second and third time—well, popped frozen burritos in the microwave.

He wanted to see her again. She wanted to see him again. Everything felt peachy. There was just that little thing about getting in touch via email. No phone numbers were exchanged, so no texting. He hadn't said where he worked. It seemed so cold and distant. It gave her an uneasy feeling.

And that brought Sara to another strange little incongruity. There was something wrong about Bryan's apartment. She just couldn't put her finger on what it was.

*

Aaaaah!

*

Sara was gripping the squeeze ball Dr. Karen had given her. "Just a little prick," said Dr. Karen. "Almost done."

Sara squeezed harder as Dr. Karen inserted a needle up behind her top lip and drove it toward her eyeball. It was exactly like a visit to her dentist, except that Dr. Karen had less technique.

"One more. You should be getting numb now."

Sara was not getting numb. She stiffened as the needle explored the area beneath her other eyeball.

"Just two more. There. That wasn't so bad, was it?"

"Well . . . " Sara felt drool drip down her chin so she stopped talking, and didn't tell Dr. Karen that in fact it was that bad.

Dr. Karen handed her a tissue. She prodded Sara's upper lip. "Feel that?" she asked.

"O," said Sara. Her tongue was numb and apparently consonants were now not possible.

"Great," said Dr. Karen.

Sara watched with horror as Dr. Karen obtained another needle. This one she knew would go into her lips. No! she thought. This is insane.

*

Aaaaah!

*

Oh, but she didn't feel a thing this time. It was as though her lips were made of cardboard. She felt like a cardboard fish, huge lips open to catch cardboard dinner swimming by. Her tongue felt like a mattress.

Dr. Karen slowly inserted the needle again and again working from the corners in.

"Aaaah!" Sara felt a twinge in the center of her top lip.

"This center area doesn't always get completely numb. I can give you more lidocaine."

"O!' said Sara. She squeezed the ball until her fingernails hurt.

"Okay, there," said Dr. Karen while peering critically at her work. "Your lips will look gorgeous. Now for the bottom and we're done."

Sara wanted to look gorgeous. She was seeing Bryan tonight. An email had come in this morning. She wasn't sure her lips would be recovered, but he had been insistent. How could she say no with another sofa pounding in sight?

He was coming by late however, very late. So she should be okay. Surely the swelling would be down by then?

"The swelling should be gone in a week or so. Keep your lips iced. And no mashing them for a few days."

Sara looked crestfallen.

"It's Friday—I hope you don't have a date tonight," Dr. Karen teased. "If you do, no kissing."

"Now for the Botox."

More needles. Dr. Karen pinched a forehead muscle and stabbed. She pinched again and stabbed.

Sara started drooling again. Getting beautiful was torture.

Sara's excuse

Ash finally answered his phone and Sara wailed, "Isth Madthy there?" she asked, her lips slapping each other like inner tubes applauding a tire show, "Can you comve over?"

"Why are you talking with a lisp?"

"Becauzhe, I hathd my lipsth dthone. They're all sthwollen and I have a dathe thonightth. Pleazhe comve over."

Ash told Sara that Maddy was there. "But I'm busy love. I'm reading *Dune* for the seventeenth time. Can't Andi help you out? I know nothing about swollen lips, beyond, you know, how to get them that way."

"Ashth! Andi'zh biszhy and I can never geth a hold ofv her all of a shuddthen."

"Okay love, stop lisping. I'll be right over."

Sara ended the call and went back to the mirror she'd been standing in front of since she'd gotten home.

She took the package of frozen green beans off her mouth. She hadn't had any frozen peas in her freezer.

She did not look like a fish. She looked like a duck. Her lips were puffed to an inch away from her teeth. Bryan was going to be here in a few hours. She tried to frown and noticed she couldn't move her eyebrows.

Well, there's one good thing, she thought. That nasty frown line between my brows isn't registering.

The doorbell rang and Sara gasped thinking Bryan had come early. She remembered Ash and opened the door.

"Bloody hell!" was his greeting.

Sara started to cry but none of her face engaged in the process. It all stayed frozen and swollen while she uttered, "Ahaw, ahaw, ahaaaaw."

"Okay darling. Come sit down." Ash led Sara to the sofa. "What did you do to your face? Don't answer that. Right. You had your lips done."

"Andth Bothoxsh."

"Botox? Is it safe? That's botulism you know."

"Ahaw, ahaw, ahaaaaw . . . "

"Okay, lay down love. I'll get some frozen peas."

Sara handed him the now half-thawed green beans.

"Right." Ash laid the limp bag on Sara's lower face tenderly. "How 'bout I make some tea?"

Sara nodded.

He came back with two cups of Earl Grey, a commodity Sara kept just for him.

"Did I hear correctly when you lisped over the phone about a date?"

Sara nodded.

"Tonight?"

Sara nodded.

"You'd better cancel. Now."

"I thriedth email—no responzhe. I don'th have histh number."

"What's his name?"

"Bryan. The guy from your sthore." Sara thought her speech was improving. The lidocaine must be wearing off.

"What's his last name?"

It had come home to Sara that she didn't know Bryan's last name the minute she had tried to look up his number. Good grief, she thought, am I naïve or just plain stupid?

"Don'th know," she admitted.

Ash narrowed his eyes. "Did you, you know . . . shag him?"

Sara glared at Ash.

"Right. Why not just tell him the truth? He was big on that as I recall."

"I'd rather keepv my enhancemenths to myshelf."

Ash petted Sara like a kitten. "Poor Sara. We'll think of something."

Sara sat up and sipped the tea, gingerly. It flowed out the side of her mouth.

"I know," said Ash, "you could just tell him you fell down and hit your face on . . . the coffee table."

Sara brightened, then slumped. "He'zh a phyzhizhisth."

"A what?"

"A phyzhizhisth. He probably knowzh the probability of that izh improbable."

"So? Tell him anyway. Then distract him with your newfound beauty. Sorry. You know I think you're dishy darling. Don't get weepy again. Being a man, it makes me want to rescue you, which I'm doing already I think."

Sara smiled at Ash and her top lip touched her nose.

"Your lips look a little better. I think the swelling's going down."

Sara touched her lips. They still felt like pillows. "I think I'm okay now. I'll take a szhower, then try to conthact Bryan again. If that failsh, there'zh alwayzh the coffee table sthory."

Ash squeezed her hand and left.

Sara took a shower and still couldn't reach Bryan. She gave it up, got dressed, and fell asleep on the sofa with a bag of mixed vegetables on her face. The green beans were fully thawed.

She awoke with a start. The doorbell was ringing. In her confusion she thought it was Ash.

Her memory kicked in before she called out for Ash to come in. She said, "Just a minute," ran to the bathroom, saw that her lips looked much better, fluffed out her hair, smelled her breath, ran to the kitchen for a mint, turned on and dimmed the dining room light, and opened the front door.

Bryan was smiling at her with blazing eyes. Before he noticed the state of her lips, she told him that she had tried to contact him.

"I fell today. Hit the coffee table." She brought the frozen veggies to her lips.

"Are you all right?" he asked as Sara waved him in and closed the door.

"Yes. I'm bruised though. I tried to cancel our date."

"I'm glad you didn't reach me." Bryan stooped to kiss her.

"I can't . . . kiss," Sara reminded him.

"How about softly, like this?" He touched her lips with his. "Let me feel your tongue."

"Bryan," Sara said after he moved to her neck and was angling her to the sofa. "What's your last name?"

"Vogel," Bryan told her while sliding his hands under her shirt.

"Where do you work?"

Between kisses to various spots but her lips he said, "Kendrick Research Labs."

"What's your cell number?"

Bryan stopped and looked at Sara. She shrunk a little not wanting too close an inspection of her face.

"Come here," he said while drawing her down to sit on the sofa. "Why all the questions?"

"When I tried to reach you I realized I knew very little about you. I didn't even know your last name."

"Well, you do now. I don't know yours either. I don't need too. I know that I like you. I know that you're hot. I know that I want to keep seeing you."

"My last name is Somers."

"How convenient to have an alliterated name being a writer. Are you sure that's not your *nom de plume*?"

They both laughed.

Sara relaxed and gave herself up to the inevitable. Why fight it? She knew they would end up having sex, so why not just go with the flow and make the most out of it?

She was not disappointed.

Andi's confession

On her way to work Monday morning Sara was forced to contemplate her new boss. She had plenty of time in which to do this, as rush hour traffic had slowed the freeway to a crawl.

Sara yanked down the visor and peered in the vanity mirror. Her lips were much less swollen and a thick layer of pinky-flesh-colored lipstick was camouflaging what was left of the bruising. She was feeling very optimistic about loving herself soon.

Back to Brittney. The bloody bitch!

How was Sara going to tolerate that witch for a boss? Brittney's lips were sewn to Mr. and Mrs. T's buttholes, and she was about to marry Greg. Sara ignored the fact that she was eternally grateful she hadn't tied herself to that cheating toad—if you could call cybersex cheating.

She had Andi for support at T-Squared. But did she? Andi was always busy all of a sudden and she was not hanging out at Booka-holic, or even being coherent. Sara thought Andi might be in love with Mr. Muscle Tone, Hans, or one of her numerous online paramours.

After grabbing a cup of awffee, Sara settled at her desk and checked emails. Brittney was looking for the layout and copy for the

City Lights newsletter. Brittney was looking for the copy for the Hadley's ad. Brittney was looking for the Future Signs revisions.

Peachy.

Sara checked her personal emails. There was one from Bryan.

"Friday night was great. You are so hot. I'm at work right now and I can't stop thinking about you. KOL . . . softly."

Sara thought, Is Bryan my soulmate? He fit Celestara's description of not being what she expected, as he was so much younger. It gave her tingles to imagine it.

Andi showed up with a smile and a croissant to share with Sara before nine-o'clock hit.

"Hey stranger," Sara said. "Haven't seen much of you lately."

"I've been in la-la land, sorry," Andi admitted. "I think I'm in love. Hans is jealous."

"So, it's not Hans. I'm seeing someone I really like too."

"Oh Sara, I'm so happy for you. Have you found your soulmate?"

"Don't know. But I've found someone a lot better than my previous boyfriend—the non-sentient partner."

Sara was baffled by the rapid change of events. How had she morphed from someone who was embarrassed to open a box containing a dildo, to someone cracking jokes about using one? Life was indeed strange.

"Hey Andi, what does capital K capital O capital L mean in a message?"

Andi blushed. "That means Kiss On Lips."

Sara took a bite of the croissant. It tasted like ambrosia. Screw Brittney. Who cared about that witch? She had other fish to fry—young, virile fish.

"Sara, I want you to meet my guy. I was thinking about bringing him to Bookaholic."

"Why don't you? That'd be fun."

"Well, he isn't really conventional in that sense. We don't really go anywhere. He likes to just be with me."

"How sweet."

"Yeah . . . you'd like Bryan."

"Bryan?"

"Yeah. I met him online in a chat room."

"About five-ten? Thin? Great-" Sara was going to say, kisser, but said, "hairstyle?"

"Yeah, actually." Andi looked confused.

"Last name Vogel?"

"Do you know Bryan?" Andi asked beaming with pride. "Then she frowned and said, "I showed him the profile we put up for you. I wonder why he didn't mention that he knew you?"

"Bloody hell," said Sara under her breath. Then to Andi, "I do know him. He probably didn't recognize me. Hey Andi, let's catch up later. I've got a long list of commands from my new boss to deal with."

"Life can be so unfair," Andi said sympathetically and left.

You have no idea, Sara thought wretchedly.

Bitch on wheels

Sara sent off two Word docs and a PDF to Brittney. She was hoping this would shut Brittney up for a while, so she could finish writing her scathing email to two-timer Bryan.

Sara's phone rang. Apparently Brittney had other ideas.

"Sara, could we have a little meeting? I'm in Kyle's old office."

It suddenly came home to Sara how much better off she'd been with Kyle as a boss. Why had she complained about him so much? Oh, life was indeed cruel and unfathomable.

Sara grabbed her little notebook and her little ballpoint pen for her little meeting with Brittney.

"Congratulations on your . . . achievement," Sara told her new boss, who was sitting importantly at Kyle's desk.

"Thank you. Now, I've been meeting with my staff to bring everyone up to speed."

Sara gripped her ballpoint pen and imagined it to be a dagger.

"I'm expecting a lot from my staff, Sara. I want to push harder for excellence. I think Mr. T realizes that he gave his son too much leeway."

"Kyle was good at his job."

"Yes, of course. But I think we can do better."

"Why did he leave?"

"Mr. T didn't say. Thanks for the Future Signs copy revisions. I want another go at Young At Heart's first radio spot Sara. It needs to be catchier, more gripping."

Catchier, more gripping, Sara wrote in her notebook concerning a diapered elderly couple hiking The Grand Canyon.

"And on another note. We are an ad agency. Our clients pay us big dollars. When they come here I want them to see everyone looking professional. I'm asking my staff to dress less casually. I want to see suits, heels . . . definitely no more tennis shoes or t-shirts."

Sara left dragging her tennis shoes on the carpet. Back at her desk she yanked down her t-shirt and threw her little notebook in the trash.

She sat and stewed, and then fished the notebook out of the trash. There was important stuff in there. Stuff such as her list of cosmetic enhancements.

Somehow Sara got through the rest of the day without seeing either Brittney or Andi again. She slipped out of the office a little early and went straight to Bookaholic.

Ash has an idea

S ara called Ash on the way to Bookaholic and told him there were strange goings-on afoot.

He asked her to pick up some food on the way. He was starving and afraid he wouldn't be able to sort out the difference between strange and normal with low blood sugar.

So Sara picked up coffee and donuts.

When she walked into Bookaholic with her purchases, she saw that the two elderly ladies were back. Well good, thought Sara. That's what they come here for—to be outraged, and tonight they won't be disappointed.

"You look fabulous. A sight better than the last time I saw you."

"Here, I brought you sugar and caffeine."

"Mmmmm. Scrummy!"

Ash ate a sprinkled donut in two bites, then reached for a long chocolate-filled one.

"I don't know how you stay so thin Ash. You don't do anything except sit around your bookstore and lollygag."

"It's the lollygagging bit that burns calories love. You should try it."

"My new boss thinks I already do. It's a cruel world that would conspire to make my ex's fiancé my boss."

"Oo hab i ee-ess ympa-ee," Ash said after stuffing the remainder of his second donut in his mouth.

"Did you just say, You have my deepest sympathy?"

Ash nodded with his cheeks filled to capacity.

"Thanks. But it isn't Brittney I came here to talk about. It's Andi."

Ash chewed up the rest of his donut and asked if she was okay.

"Yeah. But she won't be."

"Why?"

Sara bit her lip, which was not swollen anymore and looked pleasingly plumped. "You know Bryan?"

"Yeah, the guy you shagged even though you didn't know his last name."

Sara glared at Ash. "Like you've never done that?"

Ash shrugged.

"Never?"

Ash smiled wickedly, then got back to business. "What about Bryan?"

"The toad is dating Andi too. And she's fallen for him."

"Not possible."

"Possible."

"I take it then," he said, "she doesn't know you're dating him too, and that's why you're here."

"That's right," Sara told him. "Andi is so . . . sweet and innocent. I just couldn't tell her. Especially since she put him onto me."

"How?"

"She showed him my profile and told him I was her aging friend desperate for a decent date."

"That doesn't sound like Andi . . . "

"Okay," Sara admitted, "I made that part up about being old and desperate. What am I going to do? Besides sawing off his johnson and throwing it on a busy highway."

They both sat there, brooding.

"Hoist him with his own petard," Ash finally said. "I've got an idea. Let's go to the spirituality section."

The devil will get you

Sara and Ash were searching through shelves of books Ash had categorized as alternative beliefs in the spirituality section.

Sara was looking through the index of *The Only Spell Book You'll Ever Need* and Ash was rifling through *Magick Matters*.

"You'd think one of these would have a spell for impotency," complained Sara.

"You'd think."

"Look. Here's an incantation for 'imbuing the carnal lusts.'"

"How's that going to help us? Bryan seems to be doing just fine considering."

"We could reverse it?"

"Hey," Ash said, "it just occurred to me that we should be looking for curses, not spells."

"Where's Maddy when we need her? Being a vampire, she'd know about things like curses."

"She's not a vampire, love, she just dresses like one."

"God have mercy on your souls!"

Sara and Ash looked over and saw the Misses Wilson standing at the end of the aisle like two incensed gorgons.

"The devil has descended into this place."

"Almighty Lord, save these wicked heathens!"

Sara and Ash gaped. How *would* wicked heathens respond to that?

"My dear ladies," Ash said, "this is just a bit of fun."

"It's no laughing matter," Hazel Wilson proclaimed.

Perversely, this seemed to be the very thing that would indeed make both Sara and Ash laugh.

Sara coughed into her hands and Ash's face went red as he pursed his lips tightly.

"The devil will get you," said Ethel Wilson.

Having apparently been holding in too much air, Ash's lips exploded with, "I thought he was already here," much too loudly.

At this point Sara started coughing furiously.

The Lord did apparently have mercy, as the Misses Wilson left in a huff and the two blasphemers were able to vent their mirth.

Last resort

S ara and Ash were bent over Ash's desk, each with some very iffy items.

They had visited the antique shop next door and procured a mangy old Barbie doll with no clothes, and a mangy old Ken doll with frayed swimming trunks.

The mangy old Ken doll had cost a fortune, but Ash didn't care. He was bankrolling this operation and was having fun doing it.

They had turned off the store lights, locked the door, and lit some mangy old candles Ash had been saving for years in case of a blackout.

"We're supposed to have something of theirs, like a hair or finger-nail aren't we?" said Ash.

"Well, since we couldn't find a spell and we are making this up, what does it matter?"

Ash wrote BRYAN on Ken's chest. Then he drew a circle with a slash through it over Ken's unformed genitals. He added SCAMMER to Ken's back. Then added a few more choice words down the legs and arms.

Sara was frizzing Barbie's hair and drawing pimples on her face with a red marker. She dripped some candle wax on Barbie's butt and molded it into huge sagging cheeks. That was so much fun, she did the thighs too. She considered using the lighter on the Barbie boobs but wasn't at all sure that would work outside of her imagination, and was pretty sure burning plastic resulted in toxic fumes.

They both looked at the pins and then looked at each other.

"Naw," they both said shaking their heads.

"Too macabre," Sara added. "What if it works?"

"Then Brittney will have spots and bad hair," said Ash darkly, "and Bryan will get what he deserves."

They both grabbed some pins.

The candle wax had cooled and Barbie-Brittney's butt fell off.

Back to reality

With a scowl, which did not register on her Botoxed forehead, Sara adjusted her professional blouse over her professional dress pants and wriggled her toes uncomfortably in her professional dress shoes.

She'd just returned from another illuminating meeting with Brittney, who had approved of Sara's attire. On the other hand Brittney, in spite of Sara's artistic efforts, did not have pimples or bad hair this morning.

Sara looked at The High Priestess card. The High Priestess seemed to say, "What are you waiting for? Change already."

Sara rang up Andi and asked her if she could get away for a fifteen-minute awffee break.

They met in the break room.

"So how's it going with Brittney? Not too horrible I hope?" Andi said while pouring some sludge-like awffee.

"I've been contemplating taking a kickboxing class—does that answer your question? This is definitely three-sugars five-creams awffee."

Andi gave Sara a sympathetic look and dumped a packet of hot chocolate mix into her awffee.

"Hey, good idea." Sara poured an avalanche of cocoa into hers as well. "The bigger problem is paying for liposuction. Do you know any really fast ways to make several thousand dollars? All these cosmetic treatments are draining my bank account."

"No," Andi said. "But Sara, you look good the way you are. You're unique. Why try to look like a magazine model?"

"I want to look like me, when I was sixteen." Sara recalled her sixteen-year-old thighs. "Well, maybe thirteen. Don't you like my lips? And look," Sara pointed to her forehead, "no more crevice between the brows." Sara didn't add that she had an appointment scheduled for some stray pubic hair removal.

"I think you look pretty, as you always have. Have you had any more responses from your personal ad?"

"I haven't looked lately, er, too busy."

Andi was stirring her concoction and Sara sipped hers. Andi was blushing again and Sara could guess why.

"This tastes pretty good," Sara said happily. "Things are looking up."

"I haven't asked Bryan yet to come to Bookaholic with me, but-"

"I don't think that's a good idea," Sara threw in.

Andi started to ask why and Sara cut her off at the pass. "Ash has been really weird lately. I think he's going through early midlife crisis." This was not strictly a lie. Ash was always a bit off.

"Is he okay?" Andi asked with concern.

"He's just a little irritable. Maddy probably wants a day off or something unreasonable like that."

"I haven't seen Ash lately."

Andi looked guilty, but then again thought Sara, she WAS guilty of ignoring her friends while having a shag fest.

"I've got to get back before Brittney notices my prolonged absence."

"You don't think Brittney would try to fire you, do you?"

Sara chewed on that. "No," she said, "if Brittney fires me, she won't be able to lord it over me anymore."

Bryan

The scammer was arriving at eight o'clock. Sara had asked
him to come over. There were a few things she wanted to say
to him, and by way of preparing, she downed a shot of Jack
Daniels.

She considered the abhorrent nature of this love triangle. Well, it
was Andi's fault for telling Bryan about her desperate, unattached
friend. And Bryan, being the loathsome scammer looking for older
women, simply took advantage of it.

Loathsome. Not to mention hideous, vile, hateful, beastly and
slutty.

She slammed back another shot and said, "Aaargh," it burned so
badly.

When Bryan showed up with his blazing eyes, Sara almost forgot
why she had invited him.

He tried to kiss her but Sara avoided him and said, "Look, here's
the thing. You're dating one of my best friends. Her name is Andi."

"So?" Bryan said, and tried again for her lips.

"So . . . but you're seeing me."

"What's your point?"

"Well, it's . . . wrong." Sara was surprised that Bryan didn't seem in the least disconcerted. "It's weird to say the least."

"Why is it wrong? I like you. I like Andi. I like a lot of women."

"Older women you mean."

"They like me," he said. "I like sex."

Sara was processing this, thinking an insult was hidden in there somewhere, but she couldn't exactly find it.

"But, it was sneaky," Sara told him. "You took advantage of Andi's trust. How many women *do* you date?"

"Andi showed me your personal ad," Bryan admitted with a mischievous grin. "Told me she was helping you 'put yourself out there.' I thought I could be of assistance."

Sara had a good visual going of the sofa pounding.

"It's the twenty-first century Sara. We have created an electronically linked world. The technology supports people connecting as they never could before the Internet. What's wrong with me doing what I want to do? My wife doesn't mind. Why should you?"

"Wife!"

"I like you Sara. I never asked you to stop seeing other guys. Life is short—that's what all the sages say. I'm just making the most of my life."

Sara really couldn't argue with that. But a wife! Andi was going to get slammed.

Suddenly, she knew what was wrong with his apartment.

"How can you afford an apartment for your . . . liaisons? You're only twenty-four."

"Twenty-six. Money is not a problem."

Sara considered. Twenty-six, money not a problem, good-looking, no conscience. She seethed with envy.

"Bryan," Sara said after wrenching herself back to the issue at hand. "You're free to live life the way you want. But I can't see you while my friend, Andi, is dating you."

"Why not?"

"I just can't. It's too . . . complicated."

"I'll miss you then."

"You should level with Andi. Not specifically though. Not about us."

Sara wasn't sure how, when, or if she could tell Andi she'd been dating Bryan.

"Not a problem."

For you maybe, Sara thought. She wasn't so sure about Andi.

"How about one last time," Bryan asked Sara grinning. "You want it just as much as I do."

"No I don't," Sara lied, before she could change her mind.

Bryan did not look put out in the least, and Sara didn't wonder at it. Why should he, when he had a whole world of willing women waiting?

PART V
Back to the dildo

The bikini line

I t's a good thing I'm seeing my old boyfriend the hot pink dildo again instead of Bryan, thought Sara, since I wasn't allowed to shave stray pubic hairs for an entire week.

A pair of paper panties lay on the treatment chair. Sara was thinking that embarrassment plus expensive equaled not worth it.

On the other hand, she wanted to love herself, and she definitely did not love the pubic hair that had advanced below its official containment area. Whenever she shaved it, it turned into man-stubble. Hideous. And waxing it was unacceptable on so many levels.

She tried not to think about Bryan, whose body parts she missed. And she had not yet told Andi how she knew him. Oddly, Andi seemed not to be curious.

To turn her thoughts, Sara reluctantly donned the paper panties and sat in the treatment chair shivering.

Dr. Karen came in and told Sara to splay her legs. Sara did as she was told with her eyes closed, recalling the mortification she always experienced at the gynecologist.

*

Yikes!

*

Sara almost jumped out of the chair. Dr. Karen was spreading some slimy arctic-cold gel on her bikini line.

"Sorry, this gel is a little cold. Put these sunglasses on please. Now, the laser will feel like a rubber band snapping."

Sara had a vivid memory of Joey Thompson doing that very thing to her in fourth grade. It hurt like hell. And that was on her arm, not her tender inner thigh.

The laser did indeed feel like something snapping her bikini line. She sat there splayed, freezing, and gritting her teeth. The sunglasses however made it easier to ignore what she must look like in this position.

Until a nurse knocked and popped her head in. Sara just sat there, hidden behind sunglasses, mortified and exposing very personal information.

She had a moment of doubt. Was she really doing the right thing? Spending her savings on pain and embarrassment just to be attractive? So she could love herself? So her soulmate would show up?

Sara agonized over these questions as she endured the rest of the session. She had already paid for four more. She thought, I'll be happier about everything when this pubic hair falls off.

Then I will feel better about myself.

Sara gets a workout

Ash was reading *Dune Messiah* for the seventeenth time. Andi wasn't talking but Sara figured that Bryan must have leveled with her.

So, with her bank account dwindling and no liposuction in sight, she re-upped at the gym. She had nothing better to do.

The tricky part of working out at the gym was finding something decent to wear. The cottage cheese in her thighs ruled spandex out. Loose clothing made her look like someone trying to hide the fat, which she was.

She compromised with sweat pants and a spandex top. It wasn't ideal, but she fancied that at least she didn't look frumpy. From the waist up anyway.

She skipped the free analysis with a personal trainer. Her body fat percentage was not a fact she wanted to know. Nor was her weight.

Sara did not believe in weight scales. They lurked, which was impolite. They lurked in bathroom corners emanating judgment and guilt—judgment against the donuts you just ate, making you feel horrid about not exercising.

Well, Sara was exercising. She was riding the stationary bike and she was determined to stay on for twenty minutes.

After thirty seconds she was already bored and her legs felt like lead.

After one minute Sara felt as though she was climbing Mount Everest.

After one minute forty-five seconds, her butt was hurting from the hard seat and she was dripping with sweat.

She kept glancing at the wall clock, which was not registering any progress at all.

After agonies of impatience and burning thighs, Sara stopped at the three-minute mark, which, if not her goal, at least sounded official.

She wiped her brow with a complimentary towel and proceeded to the machines. While working her deflated biceps, Sara's heart skipped a beat.

She saw Kyle.

He was in the free weight section working out with an iron ball. The toad. She decided to leave before he saw her. She felt oddly betrayed by Kyle.

She went home telling herself that she would stay longer next time and really get a decent workout.

The 401k

A ngelica was making the rounds handing out checks. Sara was fidgeting in her chair with sore thighs and uncomfortable dress pants.

She envisioned a hot bath, some bath salts, candles and a glass of wine. This was the sort of thing Sara imagined would be delicious, every time she saw a protagonist in a romantic flick doing it. But in reality, after two minutes of bliss, she always got hot and sweaty and impatient to get out of the tub.

Nevertheless, sore muscles gave Sara a feeling of accomplishment. She felt empowered, thinner. She promised herself that she was definitely ramping up to five minutes on the stationary bike next time.

Angelica handed Sara the weekly reason she was at T-Squared. A call came in from Brittney who was setting up a minute-by-minute schedule for her staff while she was on her honeymoon.

Sara curled her plumped lips. Of course the world revolves around the newlyweds. When they spawn, everybody will know every last detail about their offspring's accomplishments including the first poops on the potty.

The putzes.

Sara opened her check. She looked at her 401k statement. The obvious finally occurred to her.

The Holy Grail

At Bookaholic Sara and Ash were discussing the possibilities of 401k early withdrawal. Ash was against it, as he loathed the IRS and pointed out that they would get more than Sara would.

"Not to mention the penalty love. And for what? To have your fat sucked out. What if you have it sucked out, you eat donuts, and it just fills back in? I like your thighs the way they are."

"Well I don't. If I could have thin thighs, my world would be right."

"And you would love yourself, I know. Sara, you could try just loving yourself the way you are."

"You sound like Andi."

Ash shrugged. Andi was still avoiding them. Neither of them knew why. She was either still using up all of her play time shagging Bryan, or being depressed about him because he had a wife, or both.

"So how much is the fat-sucking surgery?" Ash finally asked after picking at his nails intensely.

"Not that much. Six, seven grand. Maybe eight. I can't remember all the charges."

"I don't think they'll let you withdraw early funds unless it's for a hardship."

"This *is* a hardship!"

"Bloody hell, it is not."

"Is too."

"Is not!"

"Well, why don't you give me the money then?"

"Can't. It's tied up and I have to ask crusty old curmudgeons, in other words, the solicitors, for any of the principle."

"So you don't think they would approve liposuction for a desperate friend?"

Ash cocked an eyebrow.

Sara told Ash he was being cranky and that she was going to go to the gym to exercise, in case the 401k didn't pan out.

He stuck his nose in a book and told her she'd finally had one good idea.

While using Ash's restroom before she left, Sara considered not going to the gym as she loved being contrary. The dusty weight scales lurking in the corner however, guilted her back into it.

She kept turning the 401k idea over in her mind at the gym. She was so absorbed in imagining The Holy Grail being within reach, she actually stayed on the stationary bike for a full five minutes.

Being impatient, Sara had a real problem with the machines, which required that you do "sets." She could never get past two sets and usually only did one.

Today she did one and felt good about it, since she had reached her goal of five minutes on the bike.

On her way out of the gym she saw Kyle in the parking lot.

And this time, he saw her.

Oh, so that's what it was

Kyle beamed at Sara and asked if she was a member at this gym.

Sara couldn't help noticing Kyle's appearance, used as she was to his office attire. She furtively canvassed the contours beneath his t-shirt. Not to mention the tanned skin glistening over muscles, accented by golden hair. She was on the verge of hating him for his beauty.

She told him that she was a member, and that she had just finished her workout.

"This is serendipitous. I've been wanting to talk to you. Do you have a half hour? We could get a drink at the protein bar."

Sara agreed. She was curious to find out why Kyle had bated and then left her hanging at work. She was also happy to take this opportunity to complain about his replacement.

They sat at the protein bar and a twenty-year-old beauty with no body fat except in the exposed cleavage area waited on them. Kyle smiled at her. Of course he would.

Sara smiled at her too, through her teeth.

"Sara, I've been wanting to get in touch with you, but I'm not ready yet."

"Not ready for what?"

"I've been swamped hammering out deals. Investors, lawyers, the business plan, negotiating, putting feelers out for interest. Our business name is PopTrends. I just contracted with another startup to produce the videos. And I've hired a web developer."

"PopTrends?"

"Our interactive ad website. This is going to be big Sara. I was going to call you this week. Do you remember Ever Vessence?"

"The 'rather famous' model."

"Her father owns three cable TV stations. I've got him on the hook. He's ready to branch out. Unlike my parents."

"You mean, you tried to interest Mr. and Mrs. T with this idea and they didn't want to do it?"

"Right. They are sticking to what they know. No new blood," Kyle said without rancor. "So I quit."

"Oh. I did wonder. No one knew what happened. You were just gone one day."

"It'd been going on for some time. I've got to make my own way. They're not happy about it, but they understand."

"Have you talked to them since you left?"

"Of course. And I know who replaced me. That was my father's idea. I'm not sure my mother was thrilled."

"Neither was I," Sara admitted.

Kyle looked at Sara sympathetically. "You've got too much going for you to be pigeonholed."

Something shifted inside Sara. Here she was, talking to her old boss, the owners' son, outside of the work environment. It all seemed so different now.

She pulled her little notebook out of her purse. "Actually, after we had talked at work about your website idea, I made some notes."

"That's great. I want to bring you in on this Sara. You'd be in on the ground floor. I'm negotiating office space, but you can work from home if you want. I don't care how you do it as long as we get the work done."

Sara began to tingle with excitement. It seemed like fate. Just when her job was becoming intolerable, this new opportunity was knocking. But it was risky.

"Yes," Sara told Kyle. "I'm with you. What's your time frame?"

"I'm hoping to have this hammered out within a few months. Can you start in two? I can pay you a flat salary now, but later you can earn commissions. The potential is enormous Sara."

They discussed Sara's ideas and before they knew it, two hours had slipped by.

Office space

Sara was rearranging her condo while trying to sort out her feelings.

She was excited at the prospect of working with Kyle on a brand new business idea. On the other hand, she didn't really *know* Kyle. Her job at T-Squared was boring, irritating and sometimes hell, but it was secure and safe. Mr. and Mrs. T were stable, mature.

Kyle hung out with the likes of Ever Vessence, whom Sara suspected Kyle was shagging.

Then there was Brittney.

Sara shoved the dresser away from the wall in her spare bedroom and started pushing it aside. The bed had to go. She would sell it at a garage sale and store it in the garage in the meantime.

One good thing—she wouldn't have to go to the gym today with the workout she was getting at home.

What if this business of Kyle's didn't fly? Sara would be out of a job. She had spent a chunk of her savings on cosmetic enhancements.

Speaking of which, she had an appointment with Dr. Karen coming up for her second round of laser hair removal. Joyful prospect that it wasn't, Sara was happy about the results so far.

All in all, Sara felt that her money was well spent. She was certain she was closer to loving herself.

But The Holy Grail stood waiting to be plucked. How could she justify the cost of liposuction if she was going to take the risk of quitting T-Squared?

This was a disturbing conflict of interest.

The doorbell rang and Sara let Ash in.

"Okay love, let me at it," he said and handed her a sac with a triple latte and a cookie avalanche frap.

"Which one's mine?" she asked.

"The latte of course."

"Good luck with these instructions," Sara told him. "This desk was made in some Norwegian country."

"Right. Just when I got used to reading Hong Kong translations. Wasn't your past life somewhere in that region? Why don't you put this bloody thing together?"

Ash got busy assembling Sara's new desk. The idea of working at home had inspired her. She was creating an official home office.

Sara's phone rang. It was Andi. Sara listened while Ash read the same paragraph three times with crazed eyes.

"Andi's coming over," Sara told him as he rifled angrily through a plastic bag of nondescript hardware pieces.

"Bollocks!" he said looking up with his teeth bared, holding a scrap of metal that might or might not be a screw. "Andi's coming over?"

"Yeah, and she doesn't sound too good."

"What has our friend Bryan done now?" Ash hissed as he threw the metal scrap into the heap of other unidentifiable metal scraps.

"Jeesh Ash. I'm the one who should be pissed at Bryan, not you. Oddly, I'm not and you are."

"Bloody hell! I'm pissed at these metal bits," Ash told her.

Sara put the teakettle on.

I knew all along

The three friends were seated at Sara's kitchen table drinking tea. Ash had Earl Grey, Andi had chamomile, and Sara had PMS Tea.

"How have you been, Ash?" Andi asked him.

"Peachy."

The tension mounted. Sara informed Andi that Ash was pissed at bits of metal.

"Bloody hell," Ash said.

"I've been offered a job," Sara told Andi. She'd already regaled Ash with the whole melodrama.

"Really? What is it?"

"A startup Internet business. With Kyle."

"Kyle? You've seen Kyle? No one knew what happened to him."

Sara filled her in. She left out any references to Ever, whom she had a hate on for at the moment. She wasn't sure why, aside from the fact that Ever was drop dead gorgeous and had a rich daddy.

Ever would never have to worry over 401k early withdrawal penalties. Life was so unfair.

"What's up Andi?" Ash asked.

Sara suddenly noticed what Ash had already seen: Andi's face.

"You know Bryan don't you?" Andi asked him.

"Who?" said Ash, stalling.

"The guy I'm dating."

"Oh Bryan, right. I met him once," Ash admitted. "I don't *know* him."

"Why didn't you tell me?" Andi asked them.

"Tell you what?" they both said, puzzled yet guilty.

"You know what," Andi said to Sara.

A strained silence peppered with fear permeated the room.

"I just found out that he's married," Sara blurted out.

"I've known that all along. I'm not dumb—it's easy to tell. I mean about you." Andi was looking at Sara.

Sara was still processing the I'm-not-dumb-it's-easy-to-tell part.

Ash began, "Well, I think—"

Andi interrupted Ash and said to Sara, "Everyone wants you. Kyle wants to hire you. I'm stuck at T-Squared. Bryan thinks you're hot. And you—"

Ash's eyes were saucers.

"You think Sara is . . . smashing!"

"No I don't!"

Sara glared at Ash and Andi stood up.

"You love books and she's a writer. I'm just a lowly designer stuck in a dead-end job. I've gotta go," she said, sounding both fragile and angry.

Andi took off and after a frozen moment, Ash followed her out.

Melodrama may seem interesting from a distance, but up close it is no fun at all.

Sara was left alone at the kitchen table smarting from her friends' remarks and thoughts chasing tail in her head. She had desk parts and hardware scattered on her living room floor, and a guest bedroom torn apart.

Liposuction was hanging in the balance and she had committed to giving up a very secure job for a very risky venture.

She was no closer to finding her soulmate and her friends had gone bonkers.

Sara was wondering if loving herself was really in the cards for her.

Sara loses it

A ndi successfully avoided Sara at work the next day by concentrating with a vengeance on an adult diaper snowboarding storyboard.

Sara tried to catch Andi's eye, get her to pick up the phone, or accidentally meet up with her in the break room but finally gave up. She hadn't heard from Ash either. He'd never returned to her condo to finish the desk, and Maddy was tending Bookaholic alone this morning.

She had better things to think about anyway. Ash and Andi were welcome to their melodramas; Sara had her own to enjoy.

Instead of working on the third set of revisions for Future Signs, Sara was writing a new personal ad. With some experience under her belt, she was now equipped for the task.

"I am a work in progress with creative flair. I may like modern technology, but I'm a little old-fashioned—I'm not interested in married men, players, alternative lifestyles, or dishonesty. On the other hand, I am interested in a man who knows the grammatical difference between who and whom."

That should narrow the field, thought Sara. She rubbed her hands together gleefully and moved on to her next task.

Brittney was looking miffed but perfectly coiffed when Sara entered her office.

"Sara," Brittney began, "about the script for Young At Heart's thirty-second cable spot. They like the intro, but the closing voiceover needs work."

"Well Brittney, no problem. Excellence is something I strive for."

"Good. And, I want you at the presentation next week. Wear a suit —maybe something in cream or beige. No black."

Sara stared at her. What the bloody hell was that? Did Brittney have a degree in micromanagement, as well as her Ph.D. in ass-kissing?

"And . . . your hair. Something a little less . . . casual."

"Should I show some cleavage too? Just a professionally acceptable amount?"

Brittney seemed to awaken suddenly to Sara's sarcasm. She pressed her authority harder.

"There's no need to be sarcastic," she said. "And the Future Signs revisions. Where are they?"

"They're in my head," Sara told her. "I'll get them out of there by the end of the day." She added as an afterthought, "And into a Word doc."

"I don't appreciate your tone Sara. We are professionals here."

"You're the professional. At least, you dress like one anyway."

"Of course I do. What's going on here, Sara?"

Sara quivered. She felt out of control. She needed time to think.

"I, um."

"You need a professional cut, Sara. I'll give you the name of a good stylist."

This was too much for Sara. She said, "Don't bother. I found another job."

Brittney stared. She finally said, "What do you mean?"

"Did you lose some IQ points inhaling hairspray this morning? I'm quitting. This is my official two-week notice." Sara's heart was pounding. Did she really just say that out loud?

Brittney, very professionally, ignored the IQ bit. "You can't quit now," she said, "we're in the middle of several presentations and you are a key player."

"I thought I was just one of your little 'staff' members. When did I become a key player?"

Brittney stared, then asked if Sara was jealous.

"Of what? Your coiffure?"

"Of my position. Of my engagement."

"No I'm not. You're welcome to them both. Tell Greg to say hi to spankme2night for me."

"What are you talking about?"

"You'll find out, eventually. Two weeks. Notice. As of today."

Sara left Brittney's office with shaking knees. Elation turned into misgivings, which turned into terror.

She'd done it now. She had burned this bridge thoroughly.

PART VI
There are no accidents

The more things fall apart, the more things fall apart

Sara could not get a hold of Ash and she was trying to put her desk together herself. Maddy had no idea where he was. Sara suspected Maddy was covering for him, while he read *Children of Dune* for the seventeenth time.

The instructions looked like directions to build a particle accelerator. Sara's eyes were burning holes into the paper, which she was gripping so hard it tore.

She threw the paper down among the scattered unidentifiable hardware pieces. There was nothing there that resembled a screw. Her condo looked like a disaster area.

She had spoken with Kyle again. He couldn't pay her much for a base salary. She should have gotten that out on the table up front.

She'd had an exit interview with Mrs. T and Mrs. T was very disappointed. Sara felt guilty.

Andi wouldn't talk to her.

There weren't any responses to her latest personal ad. Not a one.

She was taking a 401k lump sum. The Holy Grail won the war against prudence. The tax on it was depressing, not to mention the penalty.

She had painted herself into a corner this time.

Since no one was around to talk to about her disastrous circum-stances, she checked her personal ad inbox one more time.

How saggy can balls get?

Finally, Sara had some responses. They were all older men.

Gary was sixty-one. His gray hair was attractive with his young-looking face. He was a divorced engineer. He liked traveling, sunsets, and reading. He was looking for an intelligent woman with a sense of humor.

White Cloud was fifty-eight. In spite of the name he looked like a man from Brooklyn with long hair. He was the author of three self-help books. He did not resonate with marriage. If Sara was interested in ancient sacred sexual techniques and a nontraditional relationship, he would love to get together.

Eric was forty-five and in obvious good shape. He owned a security business. He worked hard and played hard. He was a black belt and lived his life with honor.

Sara deleted White Cloud. She was not interested in *Kama Sutra* positions. She'd seen some of the pictures and they all looked painful.

Eric had possibilities. Not that Sara was interested in martial arts, but honor was a good thing, and the hard body was appealing.

Sara hesitated over Gary. He was quite handsome really, but he was twenty-two years older. Worst-case scenario there was Viagra she supposed. She'd never dated anyone so much older. How saggy did balls get?

She decided to call Andi who was the expert in Internet dating. Andi couldn't avoid her forever. Surely this Bryan thing would blow over. And Ash would emerge from his hibernation, and they could all be friends again.

Andi actually answered.

"Sara, I'm sorry," she said.

"You don't have to be sorry," Sara told her. "Bryan's the culprit here. I really didn't know."

"Please don't put Bryan down."

"Why? Are you still—"

"That's why I haven't been around. You all hate me."

"I don't hate you Andi, and I'm sure Ash doesn't either."

"Bryan is going to leave his wife Sara. She never cared what he did. He wants more than that."

Sara did not know how to respond to this, so she said, "That's good. I need your expertise Andi. Could you come over?"

Andi agreed, and Sara put the teakettle on. She tried to call Ash as well, thinking she might be on a roll, but he was not answering his cell phone and Maddy said he was still out.

Over tea, Sara showed Andi Gary's photo and response.

"He's good-looking." Andi said. "He sounds perfect."

"But did you see his age?"

"Of course. So?"

"Well, saggy balls. Stuff like that."

"It's what's inside that counts."

"That's easy for you to say," Sara told her. The implication here was Bryan and they both knew it. Bryan's strong points were all on the outside as far as Sara was concerned. Andi did not seem to realize it though.

"He's not that old Sara. There are a lot of really fit guys that age. I have been with older men."

"Sixties?"

"I had coffee once with a seventy-year-old man."

"Coffee is different than, you know, getting naked."

"But you don't have to get naked."

"True."

Sara decided to meet both men. Why not?

She wrote back to them while listening to Andi go on ad nauseam about Bryan's marital woes.

"What does Hans have to say about Bryan?" Sara finally asked hoping to veer Andi off the subject.

"I haven't talked to him lately, but he thinks Bryan is a scammer. He's just jealous."

"Why haven't you talked to Hans? I thought you really liked him."

Andi didn't want to say why, but finally admitted that Bryan didn't want her to. "He wants me all to himself."

Sara bit her lip and said, "It doesn't work the other way around though does it Andi? He's got a wife."

"Not for long . . . "

"Right. So what do you think about Eric?"

Eric

The High Priestess looked at Sara with warning in her eyes. She seemed to say, "You had better start loving yourself. I, being an archetype on a card may be immortal, but you are not."

Sara turned the card around and put some finishing touches to her new home office.

She had just come back from a bikini-line session. She was getting used to being exposed and humiliated—it was all part of the beautification process. Dr. Karen told her about a cheap alternative to liposuction: injections that dissolved fat. There were plastic fat wraps and cellulite massage as well.

Sara was inclined toward the real thing: lipo.

She was going to budget herself a beauty allowance. And if she didn't have enough money for food, so be it, losing weight was good too.

At seven o'clock, Sara left and drove to Juice Jazz. She was meeting Eric for some liquid dinner and conversation.

Sara reflected on her progress while checking her hair in the visor mirror. She didn't love herself yet, but she was starting to like certain isolated parts thanks to Dr. Karen. Her lips were looking particularly fine tonight with a new shade of Malibu mauve lipstick.

In spite of Sara's acquired experience meeting Internet connections in person, she was quaking inside with apprehension. What if Eric was a serial killer?

Sara had never heard of a psychotic who used martial arts as his killing method. It was usually something creepier such as baking the victim into a potpie.

So she threw that out. But what if he hated fat thighs? It seemed likely as he had chosen a juice bar to meet. If only she'd had the liposuction already.

She went to the counter and inspected the choices. There wasn't a single thing with chocolate in it.

"Sara?"

Sara turned and looked at Eric. He was exactly her height, which wasn't very much. He was, however, just as buff as his photo.

And he had a nice smile. All in all, he scored about eight-point-five. Not bad.

"Eric? Hi. Yes, I'm Sara," she said shaking hands. His grip was almost crushing.

"Have you ordered? I'll have a Greens Galore with an extra shot of wheatgrass and a protein booster."

"I think I'll have the Banana Brain Blast." Sara told the counter girl. Extra brainpower couldn't hurt when assessing soulmate potential.

"So," Sara began after they sat down, "you have a security business."

"Yes. It works right into my martial arts background. I teach specialized self-defense as part of my employees' job training."

Sara listened as Eric told her about the unique edge he had carved out for the security field.

"How long have you had your own business?"

"Twelve years with this one. I've never been an employee. I started with a hot dog stand."

Sara pointed out that he had come a long way from hot dogs to health food. Eric laughed.

"I take better care of myself now. Your body is your temple."

Sara did not want to think about her bottom-heavy temple, which was more like a pyramid, so she said, "It's risky, isn't it? Working for yourself I mean."

"It's risky. But some businesses are riskier than others. In any case, I have to be the boss—it's no fun the other way around."

Sara's mind strayed to Kyle while Eric talked about business risk. He didn't seem to notice.

She had always respected Kyle's abilities in spite of her judgments against him. She supposed it wasn't his fault he was born into a family-owned business. And he had broken off on his own. Again, she respected him for that.

"We could go now."

Sara came out of her reverie. "Go?" she said.

"To my offices. We can walk—it's just down the street."

The accident

E ric had about three thousand square feet of space. There was a training room with mats on the floor, sparring equipment, weights, and striking bags.

"I teach martial arts here too. I also train the police force in weapons self-defense."

"Do you train women too?"

"Of course. These are my black belt certificates."

Sara smiled. What could she say to such impressive titles? "Could you teach me something now?" she said. Why not just go with the flow?

"Sure. The first principal you need to know is to use your attacker's motion, don't resist it."

Eric positioned Sara on the mats and reached for her throat.

"Try and stop me from choking you. You can't pull my hands away. I'm stronger; you will lose. Now we'll do this again, and you step out and sink."

He showed her how. "Your attacker will be knocked off balance and won't be able to stop you from kicking or kneeing him in the groin. Then you run like hell."

Eric showed Sara the proper way to kick with her toes back so they wouldn't break. "Bring your knee up first, then snap kick. Use your thigh muscles, not momentum. Let's try it again."

Eric came at Sara's throat, she forgot what to do and tried to kick, stumbled and Eric caught her. The next thing she knew he had rolled them onto the mat and he was on top of her.

"You can't expect to be an expert in five minutes," Eric pointed out. Sara could feel someone's heart beating hard, but wasn't sure whose it was.

Eric kissed her. He was heavy and the floor was hard in spite of the mat. She was not sure she even wanted to be kissed, but went along with one just to score it.

Eight-point-five was holding steady.

Eric pulled her up effortlessly and swung her up in his arms.

"What are you doing?" Sara asked. "Are you made of bricks? You're really strong."

"I work out a lot."

He placed her on top of his desk and moved in close.

"Eric," Sara began, "I'm not sure—"

"I am." He kissed her again. Sara was conflicted. On the one hand, she wanted to have sex, and on the other hand, she wasn't sure she wanted to have sex with Eric.

The next thing she knew, she was having sex on a desk. Then she was having sex on a weight bench. Eric was carrying her around the room and hurling her into different positions. He may have even done a few curls with a barbell while pumping iron into her from behind.

The culminating moment came on a medicine ball. Eric drove the final thrust home and the ball slipped. Sara's head hit the floor and that was the last thing she remembered.

The nametag

Sara had a fuzzy recollection of the ride to the emergency room, featuring phantasmagorical imagery of different sexual positions interspersed with niggling anxieties about not having a job.

She came to in a white room. Eric was sitting next to her and a nurse was taking her blood pressure. She heard Eric telling the nurse what had happened. Sara tried to sink back into unconsciousness.

"She's awake. Sara? I'm a nurse. How are you feeling?"

Sara said that her head hurt.

"You have a concussion. Not a severe one. We're going to do a scan before you leave to make sure.

Sara couldn't remember if she still had insurance.

The nurse ripped off the cuff and said she would return shortly.

Eric was grinning. "Sorry Sara. I guess I got carried away. I've had concussions—you'll be fine."

"Oh good."

"I'll be right back. Got to find the restroom."

Sara said okay, and closed her eyes. She listened to the cacophony of hospital sounds: bells, buzzers, gurney wheels on scrubbed floors.

Another nurse came into her curtained area. A very pretty, very young nurse. Sara noticed the nametag. Her last name was Vogel.

It's a small world . . . too small

Nurse Patricia Vogel told Sara that she would be going to radiology in a few.

Sara saw a wedding band. She said, "I'll bet the hours are grueling here."

"Yes, I work long hours. Different shifts. But I love it." She smiled at Sara.

"Does your husband mind?"

Nurse Vogel told Sara that he didn't mind at all. "I have a very understanding husband. He's the best."

"You're lucky then."

"I am."

"What's he do?"

"Bryan's a research scientist, and busy like me. So it works out well."

"Yeah, I'll bet it does. Kids?"

"No. Bryan says he wants me all to himself for now."

Sara thought that sounded awfully familiar.

After the scan, Sara was released with a clear bill of health and a warning to take it easy for a week. Eric drove her home since driving was out of the question for her. He said he would get in touch. Sara didn't care if he did. Eight-point-fivers just didn't make the soulmate cut.

Besides, it made her tired just thinking about being with him again. If sex was that much effort, she preferred her hot pink dildo.

She called Ash. He did not answer so she left a message.

"I just got home from the emergency room. I need you."

Ash didn't call back. He showed up at Sara's door.

I still love you

Sara tried to look pissed, but her Botoxed forehead wouldn't cooperate. "Where the bloody hell have you been hiding Ash?"

"I was tending my bookstore love. How did you get a concussion?"

"I mean for the last few weeks," Sara said. "I've been fending for myself out here. And Maddy told me you weren't at your bookshop."

Ash grinned wickedly. "I've been reading *Children of Dune* for the eighteenth time."

"Seventeenth," Sara corrected.

"Okay, seventeenth. But it gets better each time, sort of like bungee jumping."

"You've never bungee jumped."

"I've read about it."

"I've needed you and you abandoned me. And Andi's no help."

"You've seen Andi?"

"Yeah," Sara told him. "And guess who else I've seen?"

"Whom."

Sara continued, "Bryan's—"

"You've seen that wanker?"

"No. I haven't seen him or his wanker. I saw his wife. She was my nurse in the emergency room."

"Not possible," said Ash, "the odds are too high."

"Possible. High odds don't mean it can't happen, Ash."

"Bloody hell. Coincidences however, may have a greater meaning. What if things, people, who are somehow connected, as you and Wanker are, Wanker and his wife, etcetera, somehow attract like cosmic magnets, and—"

"You're reading too much *Dune* Ash."

"Bollocks. But how did you find out?"

Sara told him about the nametag, and what the pretty Mrs. Vogel had said. Ash did not look happy.

He said: "Bloody hell."

"Should I tell Andi? That's what I want to know."

"Yes," Ash said unequivocally. "Tell her."

"You can help me then." Sara glanced at her watch. "She's on her way over."

"What?" Ash whined. "Now? It's, like, the middle of the night."

"Now."

When Andi arrived she was looking defensive already. Sara put the teakettle on and before Andi could be enlightened, she announced that she was getting married.

"To who?" asked Ash.

"Whom," Sara corrected him.

"Bryan asked me to marry him."

"That's probably news to his bloody wife," Ash said.

"He's getting a divorce, Ash. He wants out."

"Right. And everything on the telly is true."

Sara told the emergency room story to a gaping Andi.

"What does she look like?" Andi asked.

"You're missing the point Andi. According to his wife, Bryan's happily married. Don't you get it? He's playing you."

"No he's not," Andi said. "His wife is in denial, or pretending to strangers. That's all it is."

"Bloody hell Andi," Ash said.

Sara sipped tea and thought, Oh well, Andi is entitled to her own folly.

"I have a concussion," Sara said to lighten the conversation. "Does anybody want to hear how I got it?"

"Why do you hate Bryan?" Andi asked her friends.

Ash cocked an eyebrow and Sara shrugged.

"Look," Sara finally said, "let's just be friends again and forget about all this crap."

"I will if you will," Andi said hopefully.

"Okay," Ash agreed. "I still love you both, most of the time."

"And we love you Ash," Sara told him, "in spite of your trust fund and your hairstyle."

"What's wrong with my hairstyle?"

Sara's cell phone rang. It was Kyle.

Late night business

I
t had been a long, crazy night. First, a strenuous unsatisfactory sex scene, then the emergency room, then Ash and Andi. Then, if the night hadn't been long enough, Kyle had insisted upon meeting and Sara had used the coffee table story to explain her concussion and inability to drive.

"I know it's late Sara, but I couldn't sleep tonight without talking to you. I've wrapped the deal with Jack Crumb," Kyle told her as soon as he entered her condo.

"Who's that?"

"Ever's father."

"No wonder she changed her name," Sara said under her breath.

"This means we are a go. He's not only on board as an investor, he has a list of contacts, potential clients. We've got to get cracking. How soon until you're able to work?"

"I'm fine," Sara told him. "It was a mild concussion. It wouldn't be good for me to hit my head again, but I can work. Not tonight though."

Kyle took her hand with a grin. "Of course. Not tonight. I should let you rest. We can talk tomorrow."

"No," Sara said, "stay a while. I may be traumatized, and it may be the middle of the night, but this is great news. How about some tea, or Jack Daniels? I've got some Shiraz."

"Shiraz sounds great."

While Sara was in the kitchen, Kyle asked where her computer was located. She happily gave directions to her office, and then froze.

She froze, then had a massive hot flash—a disconcerting glimpse of what was to come when aging inexorably progressed to menopause.

Sara suddenly remembered the last time she had used George. She had decided to have non-sentient sex in another room besides the bedroom, and another position, just to shake things up a little.

George was the name she had finally bequeathed to her hot pink dildo surrogate boyfriend.

She wasn't sure she had actually put George away.

Creative types just aren't that organized, she thought desperately.

Get a grip, she told herself.

She brought drinks into her home office. Kyle was pecking away and had six tabs open.

Sara scanned the floor wildly looking for George.

"Here are a few of the prospective clients we've got major leads on. I want you to start working on 15-second to three-minute vids."

"Okay," Sara said. She pretended to inspect a spot on the carpet so she could look for George under the desk Kyle was sitting at.

While squatting, Sara saw George next to the mass of tangled wires leading to the plug strip. George must have fallen off her office chair. Surely Kyle hadn't brushed George off so he could sit there?

"You know the drill: three ideas each, one to match the current look, one slightly out of the box but very creative, very different, and one out on the edge. Let's push buttons. Start with these six."

Kyle shifted and put a foot right on George.

Sara bolted forward and said, "There's such a mess under here," while she scrambled to shove George under the wires.

"Oh," Kyle said and lifted his foot. He peered under the desk. "I can untangle these wires for you. Do you have any twist ties?"

"No!"

Sara had her hand over George but hot pink dildo was still showing. At least Kyle was looking at her now and not under the desk. Sara smiled up at him with her teeth clenched trying to say something with her eyes such as, This is making sense in a parallel dimension.

Maybe in all the wire mess and assorted paperclips and pencils on the floor, George blended in and Kyle had not noticed.

Right. Hot pink. Dildo. Bloody hell.

"No," Sara said more calmly. "We creative types thrive in chaos. Too tidy and poof . . . no good. Let's go relax in the living room."

When drowning in mortification, the only course of action is to completely ignore the situation.

"You know, Sara, if you need any 'guy' things done around your house, you can call me."

"Oh, I'm good. You don't seem the type . . . handy I mean . . . I mean, you look so good in an Italian suit."

Sara sipped Shiraz and Kyle grinned. He had dilated pupils and very sparkly eyes.

"Kyle, are you dating Ever?" Sara bit her lip. She had not meant to say that out loud.

"No," Kyle said and looked straight at Sara. "She's not my type. Why?"

"I'm sorry . . . I didn't mean to be so nosy. What is your type?" Sara would have thought Ever was every man's type. After George, what did it matter if she put her foot in her mouth? She was getting so used to embarrassment.

Kyle looked amused. "A pretty face isn't enough for me. I require something more, such as a brain."

"But I thought . . . "

"You thought wrong. I was after Jack Crumb. Ever was the contact." Kyle lifted his glass. "To our new business venture— PopTrends."

"To PopTrends," Sara said as they clinked glasses.

Kyle finished his wine and took the glass to the sink. "There. I'm going to leave now so you can get some sleep. Thanks, Sara."

Sara let Kyle out and tingled with excitement. She was starting her new job, and it was going to be fun. Not only that, tomorrow she was going to have her first cellulite massage. She could feel the fat in her thighs melting already, in preparation for being sucked out entirely.

Sara thought about the other reason she was tingling with excitement. Ever was second rate according to Kyle—how satisfying.

Before she went to bed, she washed the carpet lint off George. But George got waylaid before being tucked safely away under the socks in the dresser drawer.

PART VII
Soulmate confusion

Cottage cheese attack

All Sara had to say about cellulite massage was, "Aaah. Nnnnng. Aaaaah. Nnnnng."

She was lying on a massage table getting her fat rolled, crunched, jiggled, and squeezed. Apparently, her fat needed torture.

Sara wasn't the slightest bit embarrassed this time exposing her hideous thighs. Her masseuse was a very comfortable, very friendly, very large Nordic woman. Sara thought she may have known her during the past life in Iceland.

Her one constant thought was: Aren't massages supposed to be relaxing? Another thought was: I'm so glad I'm only getting the thighs done. And: Screw this, I'm just going straight to the liposuction.

One additional thought occurred to Sara: Why would anybody actually choose to manipulate fat for a living?

At the moment, Sara's left thigh was being jiggled so hard the wave action was making her nauseous.

"Drink plenty of water over the next twenty-four hours," the masseuse told Sara. "Toxins get stored in fat. You want to flush your system."

"But water tastes so boring. Can I drink lattes instead?"

"Coffee is a diuretic. It'll deplete the water in your body."

Sara decided to pick up some packages of Kool-Aid on the way home. If she had to drink water, she was going to put some sugar in it.

The masseuse applied a pleasant-smelling seaweed mixture to Sara's thighs and covered them in plastic wrap. Her thighs felt like two cold burritos.

While getting the facial on her thighs—the thighcial apparently—she made calculations in her head of the possibility of ramping up the beautification process. She needed more work on her face. The crow's feet were hideous.

Dr. Karen had told her about spot resurfacing. She could get rid of the crow's feet that way. There was downtime, but now that she was working at home she could do it easily.

Of course, The Holy Grail waited in the wings for her 401k to show up in one lump sum.

After the relaxing thighcial, Sara was told that there may be some slight bruising. Well, no problem she thought, George won't mind.

Her thighs were sore, but Sara had high hopes the cellulite was on its way out. She was that much closer to loving herself.

Gary

S ara put the finishing touches to her hair. It was a good hair day. Her lips looked fabulous. Her sanded and peeled skin glowed. Her bikini line was getting smooth and hairless. Her thighs felt thinner (even though her slacks did not bear this out).

She was on top of her game.

She did not think about her dwindling bank account. Why ruin a perfectly good day?

She was meeting Gary for dinner at Domo Arigatoo. Japanese food was his suggestion. Sara's knowledge of Japanese food extended to California rolls, which might be argued to be American. But, Sara was feeling gorgeous, and Japanese food sounded like an adventure.

Gary looked exactly like his photo: gray hair, attractive, young-looking face. He was tall and well built. A mature man seemed very appealing after a sub, a scammer, and a short eight-point-fiver who thought she was a dumbbell. Sara swished her cooperative hair coquettishly, liking what she saw.

After a polite greeting, they were seated at a table with eight other people. A waitress appeared to pour tea.

"*Doomo arigatoo gozaimasu,*" Gary told the beautiful waitress. She was wearing a ravishing kimono, and her flawless skin had the texture of fine porcelain. Sara had never looked good in that bright-red shade of lipstick the waitress was wearing so alluringly.

"*Doo itashimashite*," The beautiful waitress whispered with downcast eyes and dimples.

"So, you know some Japanese," Sara said to Gary.

"I speak eight languages."

Gary went on to name all the languages he knew and what dialects they were. Some he spoke fluently. Being an engineer, he was very precise about details like that.

The chef showed up and started chopping up food like a human lawn mower and cracking idiotic jokes. The waitress served sake and everyone laughed harder.

"I brushed up on my Japanese when I was there recently," Gary told Sara. "*Anata wa kirei desu yo*," he said to the smiling waitress as she poured more sake.

"What are you saying to the waitress?"

"A form of thank you. *Kanpai*!" Gary said as he held up his sake cup. "It means 'dry glass' and it is the traditional Japanese toast."

"*Kanpai*," Sara returned as she clinked her sake cup to his.

She noticed the older Asian gentleman sitting adjacent to Gary looking over with pursed lips.

"*Anata no heasutairu ga suki desu*," Gary told Sara. "I like your hair."

Good hair days were the best. "What is thank you in Japanese?" Sara asked Gary.

"The simplest way is *arigatoo*, as in the name of this restaurant."

"*Arigatoo*," Sara told him. "But, that isn't what you just said to the waitress, is it?"

"There are different ways to say everything in Japanese. In all languages."

Sara noticed the older Asian gentleman whispering to his wife.

"Language interests me; I'm a writer," Sara said.

"I love traveling. I sold my business—it was an international engineering firm—and retired early to travel for pleasure. Learning languages is a part of that love."

That bit about me being a writer must have flown right over Gary's head, Sara thought with slits-for-eyes.

"So where are the best sunsets?" She asked, referring to his personal ad.

"On the west coast of Costa Rica, over the ocean. Costa Rica is *muy hermoso*. Very—"

"Very beautiful," Sara finished for him. "I recall a bit of my high school Spanish." She had meant the statement as a joke, but Gary's smile made her feel like a clumsy third-grader receiving accolades from a college professor.

The beautiful waitress was refilling Gary's teacup. Her lovely dimples were showing.

"*Boku to dekakenai*," Gary said, apparently thanking her again in yet another phrase.

The waitress did not answer, but smiled shyly and cast her eyes down even lower.

The old Asian gentleman's lips were pursed again, while glancing over at them in short clips, staccato fashion.

The chef's joke's were getting sillier, while he flipped food onto plates, sometimes missing. Sara thought bibs would have been a good idea considering.

Bowls of rice were served and Sara tried using the chopsticks. She had never been very good at it. Gary seemed to be fluent in that too, wielding his with flair.

Sara stuck her chopsticks in her bowl of rice and reached for the sake cup.

Gary reached over and said, "Excuse me." He pulled out the chopsticks and set them on a little dish Sara thought was used for sauce. "Never put your *hashi*—your chopsticks—in your bowl like that, unless you're at a funeral. They rest on the *hashi-oki*."

"Oh, thank you. I mean, *arigatoo*."

The chef lit someone's dinner on fire after constructing a temple with chicken and vegetables.

More sake was poured. Sara met her neighbor, a bald-headed Car Zone manager visiting from Minnesota and his wife who loved crafting. She taught Sara how to make painted gourd flowerpots in ten easy steps. Gary taught everyone at the table to say *kanpai*!

The sake was making Sara feel very warm and fuzzy.

Gary carried on quite a conversation with the waitress while settling the bill. On the way out of the restaurant, the older Asian gentleman tapped Sara on the shoulder. Gary had gone to use the restroom.

"Please excuse me," he said. "Is that man your husband?"

"No," said Sara, "he's just my date."

"Please excuse me. Your date was wooing our waitress. He asked to take her to dinner. It is not respectful. I thought you should know."

Sara stared at him. "*Arigatoo*," she said finally.

"*Doo itashimashite*," the man said while bowing.

Oops

"The toad. The bloody toad! What did you say to him?"

Ash poured two more shots of J. D. and Sara slammed hers down.

"Nothing. I just walked out of the restaurant while he was in the restroom. I'm sure he noticed my absence at some point. Gee, I hope he hadn't already popped the Viagra—what a waste."

"Poor darling," Ash said while massaging Sara's neck.

"I'm so screwed. Men don't work out for me. What's wrong with me Ash?"

"Nothing. You're smashing. It's these American blokes who are all wankers. We British blokes—"

"I know, you have lower standards."

Ash was sidetracked by an overweight, middle-aged woman with a stack of dog-eared romance novels to check out. Sara looked at the muscle-bound heroes on the covers. She imagined herself eating tubs of ice cream while pretending to be the captive of a handsome pirate.

Tears filled Sara's eyes. What was there to look forward to? The Einsteinian relativistic age reversal had happened long ago, and she was left with paintings of roguish men on book covers and George.

Ash turned back to Sara and said, "I don't have lower standards . . . are you crying?"

"No," Sara told him as the tears spilled down her cheeks. "Do you have a tissue?"

Ash retrieved a wad of toilet paper from his restroom.

"Maybe I should try women," Sara said after blowing her nose.

"Can I watch?" Ash asked with a grin, and slammed another shot.

Sara heard shuffling in the cookbook aisle and looked over to see the Misses Wilson peeking around the corner. Ethel and Hazel, who had nothing left in their lives but outrage at those who were doing what they most probably longed to still be doing themselves.

"Ahaw, ahaw, ahaaaaw . . . "

"Sara, come here love." Ash pulled Sara into his arms and petted her like a kitten. He smelled good. Sara melted into his arms thinking that Ash was probably her last chance for male contact of any kind.

Ash was strong and very male in spite of his propensity to lollygag and get no exercise whatsoever. Sara was reminded that he had very attractive brown eyes and a kind nature. Not to mention a rakish hairstyle, which fit nicely with the romance novel persona suitable for old women with no chance of real sex.

The next thing she knew, she was kissing Ash. Ash was kissing her back. His lips were rather yummy and before she could score the kiss she heard a gasp.

The Misses Wilson were standing at the cookbook aisle end in postures of shock. But they weren't the only ones witnessing the kiss.

Maddy was staring silently from the sci-fi section.

And Andi had just come in the door. She was holding a bottle of wine, and looked ready to burst into tears.

Retreat when you're losing

Sara decided to concentrate on work. She was sick of dating. She was on Andi's shit list. And she was embarrassed about Ash.

Ash had chased after Andi, who very melodramatically had run out of Bookaholic after seeing her friends kissing.

Maddy had merely shrugged her shoulders and slunk away, while the Misses Wilson had left in a huff, which of course was the way they loved to leave.

Sara had scored that kiss a nine-point-seven.

She was attempting to ignore it however, as it opened too many cans of worms.

It was heaven working at home. She could wear pajamas, not do her hair, drink good coffee, and eat all day long. Which also made it hell. She could feel the cottage cheese multiplying happily and unfettered in her thighs.

On the other hand, her level of creativity soared without the distractions of a noisy corporate office. She got into the groove and was doing the best work of her life.

Kyle came over and was wowed by what she had come up with. He was more excited than ever.

They got online and surfed video spots for competition.

"Check it out, Sara."

Kyle had found a Young At Heart spot.

"I'm Free," sang a no-name band trying to sound like The Who. "I'm free! And I'm waiting for you to follow me," the band continued, while an attractive elderly couple bicycled along a beautiful section of west coast highway wearing adult diapers.

"I wonder if he's wearing the stripes," Sara said.

"And she's wearing the thong."

Kyle and Sara laughed so hard they cried.

"This is so much better than working at T-Squared, no offense to your parents," Sara said.

"None taken. Hey, do you want to meet up at the gym tonight? I'll be there around six."

"Sure," Sara said, "I think I need a workout. I'm getting butt-spread worse than ever working at home. It's the easy access to a refrigerator full of sugar-laden desserts."

"Your butt matches the rest of you. What I mean is, it looks fine to me. I'll see you at six then."

And Kyle left. What the hell did he mean? Well of course, her butt matched her thighs. She could not imagine he liked her cottage cheese deposits.

Sara went to her bedroom mirror and inspected her butt. It did not look fine to her.

Sleight of fat

K yle was showing Sara how to swing an iron ball he called a kettle bell. They were in the free weights room at the gym. Sara had to admire Kyle's muscles. She thought it was unfair that men could build muscle tissue so much more easily than women. Women were better at building fat.

They were standing in front of a wall mirror. Sara was trying to avoid looking in the mirror, the same way she did at department stores when trying on bathing suits. The trick was to only see the parts of her body she liked, and not notice the parts she didn't like.

She called it "sleight of fat."

What was driving her crazy at the moment were her crow's feet, which she could see now even from a distance when she smiled or laughed. Trying not to smile was difficult around Kyle. They seemed to be on the same humor wavelength.

So when he was explaining how to align her body, Sara was plotting the resurfacing of her eyes. She had considered more Botox, but a face frozen from the nose up just did not appeal to her.

"Swing like this," Kyle told her. He swung the iron ball up in front of him and back down between his legs.

Sara had a smaller kettle bell that Kyle had chosen for her. She tried swinging it and almost fell forward. Kyle caught her and repositioned her body, explaining where to shift her weight.

He had his hands on her waist and back as she tried again.

"Good," he told her. "Keep your chin up. That's great."

When Sara finished with a set of ten swings, Kyle gave her a sideways hug. She looked up and his smile was dazzling.

Was it her imagination that sparks were flying?

No, can't be, Sara decided.

But on the way out to the parking lot, Kyle gave her another hug. And another dazzling smile.

Laser resurfacing

Sara sat in front of her TV with a bowl of ice water. The skin around her eyes felt like boiling plutonium.

She was dipping a cloth into the ice water and laying it over her eyes, listening to some poor sap on a talk show explain how he had burst his stomach after gastric bypass surgery by gorging. After eleven more surgeries, he was now back up to four hundred pounds.

The resurfacing had been pretty easy. Dr. Karen had glopped on a numbing gel and washed it off after it had taken effect. The laser zapped the skin cells, which were vacuumed up by an assistant. The worst part was that Sara could smell her cooked cells like burnt pork roast, except the smell had that human quality.

It gave her the creeps, especially since it was her own face cooking.

"You'll be gorgeous," Dr. Karen had said. "But you'll look sunburned around the eyes for a few days. That's after the oozing."

There was nothing Sara liked better than to ooze.

"I sued my doctor for twenty million," the talk show guest said. "It wasn't my fault the staples burst. I have an eating disorder for heaven's sake. I wasn't properly screened."

Sara considered the sum of twenty million dollars. What would she do with it?

1. She would get liposuction immediately.
2. She would get veneers on all her teeth.
3. She would hire cabana boys for her new home with a pool, and sex would never be a problem again.
4. She would hobnob with celebrities and find out all their secrets to staying young, beautiful, and cottage cheese-free.

Sara realized that with twenty million, she could definitely love herself. Even ten million.

Heck, she would settle for one million. She bargained with God. God, if you'll give me just one million dollars, I'll volunteer to give vaccinations to rural African children.

Or, I'll help PETA clean up oil spills. Whatever you want, God.

Sara had driven home from Skintastic wearing a pair of owl-sized sunglasses. She had skipped the painkiller they offered, as that would have rendered her unable to drive. Sara currently had no friends available for the task. Ash was making himself scarce again. Andi hated her apparently. And she didn't want Kyle seeing her like this.

Sara considered Ash. She couldn't help wondering what sex with him would be like after the nine-point-seven kiss.

But then, there was Kyle . . .

Sara was taking a few days off. She would be seeing Kyle after that.

She wanted to find out if the sparks were still flying.

Ooze

Sara oozed for two days. It was not pretty.

It was a good thing she had stocked up on staples such as chocolate, cookies, and ice cream. She didn't go out the door, nor did she answer it.

She spent her time watching soap operas and talk shows. Daytime television was a black hole that sucked her into a world of living vicariously through an endless parade of melodramatic idiots.

Sara emerged from the black hole when she discovered a vintage cable station that ran old episodes of I Love Lucy with Ricky Ricardo.

She thought of Ever's father, who owned a cable station. She wasted some time thinking of reasons why she hated Ever.

She expanded her list of how to spend a million dollars.

She thought about Kyle's sparks, Ash's kiss, and Bryan's sofa pounding.

She trimmed her toenails.

George got a lot of action.

She checked her personal ad. She had seventeen messages.

Nine were from Gary. Sara didn't bother reading any of those. Gary could console himself with the beautiful Asian waitress.

One from Eric:

> *Hey. How's the head? I am considered lethal, you know.*
> *Let's get together for some more self-defense lessons*
> *lol. Seriously . . . let's.*

One from Todd, the sub:

> *My queen, my priestess, pleasing you is my desire. I*
> *have been very naughty thinking about you. I await*
> *your punishment. Spanking is not good enough—*

Sara pounded the delete key.

She had three messages from Bryan. They all sounded as though there had never been any conversation at all about Andi, his wife, and not dating. He was still playing her. The toad!

Delete. Delete. Delete!

One was from White Cloud in spite of the fact that Sara had selected "not interested":

> *Beautiful lady, my spiritual journey has led me down*
> *exciting new paths. I have chronicled my latest*
> *metaphysical discoveries in my new book,* Soaring
> With The Eagles—

Sara considered soliciting White Cloud for a video spot, but decided to delete him.

Two were new contacts.

Dave:

> *ur so sexy. i luv smart womin. do u hav a webcam?*

Delete.

Jumok:

> *I would love to meet you. I am in Kenya working until I*
> *transfer to Texas. And when I get my green card—*

Delete.

Did these guys even read what she wrote?

At the moment, Eric was looking pretty damn good.

But, Sara remembered that she was sick of dating.

She wrote back to Eric:

> *"I'm not sure I can withstand another lesson lol. My head is fine. No permanent damage, aside from the lobotomy they performed after the MRI was consulted."*

She shut down her computer and oozed some more while watching Lucy and Ethel wrap chocolates in a candy factory.

Sparks fly like crazy

Raccoon eyes weren't as bad as ooze, Sara told herself. She looked as though she had gotten a reverse burn at the tanning parlor: her skin was red where the goggles should have been.

She was back to work a day early, having reached the end of the ooze and having nothing better to do. She was sick of daytime television.

She'd hit a snag on an Italian ice cream business called Gelato Squisito. The name just did not lend itself to any visuals besides Italian men squeezing women's butts, or ice cream with squid in it.

She was researching gelato sites when a text came in. It was Kyle.

I'm walking up to your door. Is this a bad time?"

*

Crap!

*

Sara couldn't say she wasn't there. Kyle would have seen her car parked outside since her garage was now full of her spare bedroom.

She put on a pair of sunglasses and opened the door.

"Hey Kyle, I was just going out to the grocery store."

"In your pajamas?"

"Um . . . " Sara looked down and confirmed that she did indeed have pajama bottoms on. But her t-shirt was perfectly suitable for daywear.

Sara decided to ignore the grocery store bit, which wasn't working, and invited him in.

"We've got office space," Kyle said. "There'll be some renovations before we can move in. I want you to come down and tell me what you want for your office. You can still work from here if you want, but there'll be space for you there to land."

"You're so . . . thank you." Sara was at a loss. She must have had other past lives aside from the Viking slut life where she'd done something right.

"In the meantime, I'm having a client get-together at my place. We'll have an office opening later. Are you going to leave your sunglasses on?"

"Well . . . yes. I've got . . . allergies, and my eyes are sensitive to light."

"So, you didn't have laser resurfacing done, or an acid peel, or blepharoplasty or something?"

Sara froze. "You mean eyelid surgery? No. It's just allergies. Oh, okay. I did have resurfacing done." Sara whipped off her sunglasses feeling that Kyle would have figured out she was lying eventually. "How did you know?"

"My mother. She's had all sorts of things done. You're just pink now. You'll be good in a couple of days."

"Okay, doctor Kyle."

"It's cool. Cosmetic surgeries and all."

"You're mother just tells you about her . . . upkeep?"

"Well, we are a close family and it's not like she can hide it from me. She's thinks it would be bad karma."

"Really. She believes in reincarnation?"

"Yep."

Sara was taking this information in. It was amazing really, how you could work side-by-side with people and know so little about them. On the other hand, Mrs. T was a baby-boomer, and the baby-boomers had invented the new-age movement.

"Well, I'm glad you don't mind my pink eyes, since you forced your way in here."

She was still trying to get over her exposure and embarrassment.

"No problem. But, I'm not sure why you had it done."

"Crow's feet. Why else?"

She couldn't believe she was having this conversation.

"Crow's feet are a good thing; they are evidence that you smile."

"And I've heard people say that gray hair is attractive. But do you see any women with gray hair on the 'top ten sexiest women' list?"

"But you don't have gray hair."

Sara started to say, Yes I do but I dye it you idiot, and said instead, "That's not the point."

"What I'm trying to say is, you're sexy to me."

Sara fidgeted. She did not want to meet Kyle's eyes. Especially with her pink-rimmed ones.

"Anyway, Friday night. Six o'clock. I don't think you've been to my house. I'll text you the address."

They talked some more about the client base and the potential for growth and Sara walked Kyle to the door.

"Thanks for everything Sara. I couldn't do this without you." He hugged her tightly . . . for a long time . . . and Sara felt sparks flying like crazy between them.

Kyle's house

Sara's usual disdain for business parties was curiously absent as she did her hair. She was actually looking forward to this one.

Her thighs were still full of cottage cheese, but her raccoon eyes were now blending into the rest of her face. The Botox was keeping her forehead smooth, her lips were looking nicely gorged, and her bikini line was almost maintenance free. Life was good.

Moreover, this business party was for a business she cared about. It gave her a sense of purpose. She felt ready to conquer the world.

And then there was Kyle.

After adding the finishing touches to her hair, Sara pulled on the new dress she had purchased that day. Oddly, now that she was counting pennies, she was spending more money than ever.

However, the dress looked great, as long as Sara only looked at the parts of her body she liked. She pulled on a pair of silvery pumps, and waltzed out the door.

Kyle lived in a nice part of town in a custom home area. His street was full of cars when Sara pulled up. The front yard was beautifully lit with colorful ground lights.

Ever answered the door.

Why was Ever answering the door?

Sara smiled at Ever with her lips only. Ever looked stunning. She had no fat cells to ignore. Her Barbie doll legs were three miles long. Her veneered teeth sparkled through a Hollywood smile, and her face was framed by platinum blonde hair that fell like fine silk over her bare tanned shoulders. Her breast implants were showcased in a low-cut dress that could not have comprised more than an eighth of a yard of slinky material.

Sara felt the cottage cheese in her thighs quivering with self-loathing. She felt her hair frizzing. She felt short. She felt fat. She felt her bikini line itching where the stray pubic hairs were trying to grow back. She felt the skin around her eyes heating up and turning red again. Thanks to the Botox however, none of this registered on Sara's forehead.

Sara did not ask Ever where Kyle was. She waddled away and went for the bar.

At the bar, Sara downed a shot of spiced rum and resisted uttering a string of expletives.

Screw Ever. Sara was going to hold her chin up and concentrate on her Plan instead of Ever's undeniable beauty.

Liposuction was happening just as soon as she had that 401k check. So were veneers. She would just spend her stash and not look back.

Sara spotted Kyle talking to a couple of bald men in suits. They both looked successful and wealthy. Sara wondered why neither of them had had hair transplants.

But then again, in an unfair world, men with fat wallets could be sexually attractive without any claims to good looks.

She caught Kyle's eye and smiled—this time with her whole face. Kyle's answering smile seemed to light up the whole room. He motioned Sara over.

Kyle introduced her to John Bingham and Chad Larsen of Bipartisan Counterpoint, a political cable talk show. John was the republican and Chad the democrat.

"Sara is the creative talent at PopTrends," Kyle told the bald men. They looked her up and down, assessing her talent apparently.

"So, which side of the aisle are you on?" asked John.

"I thought it was taboo to talk politics at a party," Sara said, as Kyle was drawn away with an apologetic glance.

"Nicely avoided," Chad said. "Have you thought about a political career?"

Sara was desperately calculating how to escape before she was forced to admit that she had written in "Mickey Mouse" as her presidential vote last election.

It seemed like hours of hobnobbing before she could talk with Kyle again. Hobnobbing was, of course, the reason for the party. But Sara had lost her desire to hobnob and it was Ever's fault.

"You're much better at this sort of thing than me," she told Kyle. "We creative types are notoriously bad at sales."

"Just throw a wink or two, and look pretty. I'll do the rest."

"So, how're we doing so far?"

"Great. You'd better be prepared for a slew of work coming down the pipes in the next few weeks."

"No problem, as long as I can work in my pajamas."

Kyle smiled with enough wattage to light up New York, then excused himself to continue mingling.

After an exhausting game of talking to, while avoiding physical contact with, Angelo Mantissi, owner of Gelato Squisito, Sara went to the backyard for some fresh air. It too was beautifully lit, including a sparkling pool with floating candles. The crowd had spilled out here but Sara found the atmosphere more intimate than inside the house.

The air was cool and refreshing. A gibbous moon was just rising like a drunken disk of cheese. Sara was exhausted from mingling. She fell into a patio chair and closed her eyes. For some odd reason she heard Celestara telling her, "This is why you sabotage your relationships now. You feel you don't deserve to be loved."

Why on Earth was she thinking about that?

She looked nervously around the crowd for Celestara.

Celestara was not there. Sara put it out of her mind and closed her eyes again. She'd rather plan her next visit to the dentist to ask about veneers. It occurred to Sara that she might ask her dentist to do a trade for ad copy.

Sara wondered if Dr. Karen would suck out the cottage cheese from her thighs in exchange for a spot on PopTrends.

With these cheerful thoughts in her head, Sara opened her eyes. What she saw was not pretty.

To be honest, it was pretty, but not to Sara.

She saw Ever and Kyle kissing under the palm tree.

Unplugged

S ara dipped a potato chip in her bowl of chocolate ice cream. The trick was to eat the chip before it got soggy from the ice cream, but not so fast the ice cream froze her brain.

She had a good rhythm going. The chips needed to be broken in half. The dip needed to be small. The chewing had to happen on both sides of her mouth while some of the ice cream floated on the middle of her tongue.

It was very satisfying figuring out the logistics of such a complex and difficult operation.

It occurred to her that if she microwaved some chocolate chips and mixed them into the ice cream before dipping, then the consistency and temperature might be even better. On her way to the kitchen to test her theory, the doorbell rang.

She ignored it and rummaged in the pantry for the chocolate chips.

"Sara, open the bloody door," she heard Ash say while knocking hard.

"No," she yelled, loudly enough for him to hear.

"All right then. I'll have to use my key."

Sara went to the door and said, "Crap. I did give you a key, didn't I? Why did I do that?"

"Because, love, you locked yourself out last year and had to hire a locksmith. Remember?"

Sara opened the door. "Yes, I remember. Give it back. I want to wallow and you're not letting me."

"Wallow . . . what's happened now?"

Sara didn't know. She'd seen Kyle kissing Ever. The next thing she knew, she had left and was driving home in tears.

She'd let the battery die on her cell phone and hadn't checked email. After that, chocolate had become a destination.

"Nothing's happened," she told Ash. "I just have PMS. So you'd better be nice to me or I'll scratch your eyes out."

"Are you out of your PMS tea?"

"Why are you here Ash?"

"Okay. You know . . . when we kissed . . . "

Sara was feeling reckless. Or perhaps it was the rush of endorphins released from all the chocolate. "You mean—"

She grabbed him and kissed him. It was a rather chocolaty kiss.

Sara had heard a phrase, Friends With Benefits. She considered. Ash would be a nice break from George.

"Darling," Ash said as he stroked her cheek. "I came here to—"

"Have you heard of Friends With Benefits?" said Sara.

Before Ash had a chance to answer, she pushed him away.

Sara was looking at her door, which she had neglected to close. Kyle was standing there.

"I've been trying to reach you," Kyle said flatly. "For hours. And hours."

"Hours?" Sara said, stalling for time to get clear on what exactly was happening.

Right. She had bailed on the business party. Kyle was shagging a skinny model and had lied about it. He had just witnessed her contemplating sex with her best friend. Aside from those important bits, there was the fact that he was her business partner and she had not been taking his calls.

"Um," was all Sara could think of to say.

"I'll just come back another time," said Ash.

"No," said Sara while gripping Ash's arm. And to Kyle: "I thought you weren't dating Ever."

"I'm not," Kyle told her. "And who are you?" he said to Ash.

"Ash Bennett," he said extending his hand. "I own a little bookstore on—"

"The Gelato Squisito account is solid. We need two spots roughed out by the end of the month."

"I'm on it," said Sara flatly.

"I'm not dating Ever."

"Right. I'll get right on those scripts."

"I'm leaving now," said Ash.

"No," said Sara as she pulled him into her.

Then she froze.

And stared.

And squinted.

And stared.

Limping up to her door on crutches was a man she never thought to see again.

His long hair was pulled back in a ponytail, his rakish smile was shy and bold at the same time, and his leg was apparently broken.

Excerpt from Sara's romantic interlude

"Wow, I really missed you," Night whispered into Sara's hair.

"When did you get back in town?" Sara asked, trying to ignore the weakness in her knees. Night looked the same, except for a few crow's feet, which incidentally looked great on him but hideous on her.

"Three hours ago, no four, I don't know," Night answered, "as long as it takes to get here from the border."

Sara had the presence to say, "It's a good thing I haven't moved," while Night deposited wet fire blossoms on her neck and shoulders.

Night's next kiss started out soft, but grew exponentially in passion until Sara's weak knees turned to delicious butter. Sara didn't realize her shirt was off until Night unhooked her bra. Her nipples were like racing swimmers on the edge of the pool, waiting to plunge into Night's mouth.

"I'd carry you to the bed babe, but my leg's broken."

"Let me help you hobble," Sara breathed, leading her long-lost lover to the sacred temple of cosmic soulmate lovemaking.

Night's nine-point-nine-and-three-quarters kisses just kept coming, and coming, along with the impassioned caresses Sara had so missed since he left. Night became completely focused and absorbed by whatever he was doing, and sex was no exception.

Sara swooned, but luckily she was lying on the bed and didn't fall down anywhere.

A broken leg did not hamper Night's repertoire of sexual positions; there were countless intimate couplings possible still. When the first culminating moment came, and Sara was quaking with ecstasy, she looked into Night's eyes and knew.

He was the one.

PART VIII
A new look at an old flame

More sex with a sentient partner

In times of profound confusion, default to the familiar.

Sara made coffee for her soulmate, and thought of Angelica. She thought of T-Squared. And that led her back to Kyle.

Thinking of Kyle gave her a little twinge. He was perfectly polite. They did not talk about Ever. It was strictly business now.

Back to her soulmate. It was obvious. Night was her soulmate. Hadn't she always been head-over-heels for him? He had returned to her, and it seemed as if no time had passed.

"Do you have any goat's milk?" Night asked.

"N-no. Afraid not. But I have yak butter. Just kidding."

Night kissed the back of Sara's neck. Night was bar none the most virile man Sara had ever known. He seemed indefatigable.

He had just returned from California, where he had stopped on his way back from Tibet. He had run out of money and worked for a while as a snowboard instructor at Tahoe. It was there that he was turned on to snowkiting, and had broken his leg.

"Worth every ounce of pain," he told Sara.

This information had put a tiny damper on Sara's joy. She thought Night had come to her directly from the Himalayas. A sidetrack in

California, complete with Hollywood Barbie Dolls dressed up as snow bunnies dampened the romance-novel quality of his return.

However, they had shagged so many times in the last few days Sara was finding it difficult to stand, or even think.

She reflected that it was a good thing she was working at home in this condition. That brought her back to T-Squared and Kyle.

Apparently cow's milk was okay, as Night had a mixing bowl heaped with cereal and was pouring half the container into it.

"Going to the rock-climbing gym today. Wanna go?" he said between huge mouthfuls.

"You're leg is broken."

"I'll campus on belay."

"What's that?"

"Arms only. On rope. I need to train grip."

That would work for Sara, since her trembling legs were useless. However, she was going to the new offices this morning, and had an appointment with Dr. Karen in the afternoon.

"That's cool," Night said genially while scanning a local lifestyle rag. As soon as he emptied the bowl, he made another one. "There's a disc golf tournament this weekend."

"I may have to work," Sara told him apologetically. She just could not take a sport that involved Frisbees seriously.

"That's cool," Night told her.

Sara took a cup of coffee into her office. She didn't bother making the bed. With Night there, it was an exercise in futility.

She checked her personal ad inbox before writing the voiceover for Bipartisan Counterpoint.

White Cloud was inviting her to his book signing.

Delete.

Dave:

"ur so sexy. i luv smart womin. do u hav a webcam?"

Okay, that was either déjà vu, or Dave had a bulk mail operation and was counting on sheer numbers to land a date (if you could call webcam sex a date).

Delete.

One from Eric reminding her that she needed a lesson in self-defense. None from Gary.

Sara considered. Night would probably like Eric. They could cross-train together.

Todd was still being naughty and needed spanking.

One new contact, Ralph, whose photo looked exactly like Robert Downey Jr.:

> *"I would like to take you on a Caribbean cruise. I'm*
> *financially independent and own three*
> *businesses—"*

Right. Delete.

And, one from Bryan. Sara sighed and opened it.

> *"Miss you—B"*

Sara bit her lip, feeling herself start to cave. Damn, that guy was good.

New digs

Sara walked into two thousand square feet of PopTrends office space. Kyle had insisted that impressive digs were necessary to hook the big clients. It was an investment.

The floors were painted concrete. The furniture was European modern. She heard someone pecking on a computer, and walked toward Kyle's office.

"Hey, Kyle," she said as she entered his office, "it's looking great."

"We're ready for our office opening." Kyle swung around in his ergonomic chair. He was smiling. "I'm looking to hire a receptionist to field calls and set appointments."

"Great." Sara pictured Ever's platinum-blonde leggy look-alike.

"This guy might work." He handed Sara a resume. "He has sales experience and can also be selling. We'll have to double up like that at first."

"My sales skills are nonexistent."

"Not you. You are the whole creative department. Your office is next to mine."

They went into the office next to Kyle's. It was furnished with the same ergonomic chair and furniture.

"I got you a laptop. That way you can take it home if you want. Everything's networked. How are the Crumb Cable spots coming?"

Sara was having a difficult time with this project. She couldn't keep her hate on for Ever out of her mind while trying to write ingenious scripts for Ever's father.

Then there was Night. Working at home had become complicated now that Night was there. Sara wondered if he was going to get a job anytime soon. He was currently living off money saved from his Tahoe gig.

"I'm working on it," Sara told him, while thinking how she would decorate her new office. "Some projects are harder than others."

"We need this Sara. Jack Crumb's account is our primary foot-in. His spots have to sing."

Yeah, thought Sara, sing. We must keep Ever's father happy.

"We're in this together," Kyle said as he stood up and put his hands on Sara's shoulders. "We have to do whatever it takes to make this business happen. Are you with me on this?"

"Yes," Sara told him as she looked into his eyes. "I'm with you."

Kyle held her eyes for a few seconds as though to impart some silent message, and let go of her shoulders.

After checking out her new laptop and ergonomic chair, Sara decided to have lunch at Bookaholic. She felt she needed to clear things up with Ash. Now that she was with Night again, Friends With Benefits was out of the question.

On the way to Bookaholic, Sara picked up sandwiches.

Ménage à trois

"Ash, stop eating those donuts and have a sandwich."

Ash looked up at Sara with his cheeks stuffed. When he smiled he looked like a hamster. "Oh-hay," he said through a small O-shaped opening and spewed a dusting of powdered sugar at Sara.

This made him laugh, which resulted in more powdered spew.

He put the donut bag in his top drawer and reached for the sandwich.

"How do you stay so thin? It's not fair."

"Life is not fair, Sara. That's what makes it so interesting."

"Yeah, if you're ectomorphic and have a rich daddy, like you. Try being almost forty, endomorphic, and financially challenged."

"My daddy's not that rich. My uncle is. He's been knighted. And who's forty by the way?"

Ash took a bite of the sandwich a hippo would admire.

"Ash, about our kisses."

Ash smiled again with his cheeks stuffed.

Sara heard shuffling in the gardening aisle. Did the Misses Wilson *live* at Bookaholic?

"I know," Ash said through various sandwich ingredients. "You're busy with Gimpy. But, remember when you mentioned the lovely phrase, Friends With Benefits?"

For a brief moment Sara wondered what Ash looked like with his clothes off. He probably had no muscle tone whatsoever. It was the Australian dudes who were buff and had those manly outback accents.

"Ash, let's put those kisses behind us."

"You want me to kiss your behind? Brilliant!"

"Ash!"

"Actually, those kisses got me thinking. How about a ménage à trois? The Frenchies do it and it works for them."

"With who?"

"Whom. Andi of course. Not Gimpy." Ash lowered his voice to a loud whisper. "Okay, if you want Gimpy in, I could do him. We're all friends so it should work out swimmingly."

The visuals Sara got from this suggestion nearly made her crazy.

"Ash—are you nuts? No. I couldn't *do* Andi. You're not serious? And since when are you bisexual?"

"I'm not anything in particular, darling. I just like sex. It comes in many forms. Pun intended."

"Andi isn't even talking to us," Sara noted. Her unruly imagination was still trying to conjure up visuals of Night and Ash "doing it."

"That could be remedied darling. Leave it to me. Or," Ash lowered his voice to a whisper, "there's always Maddy. She's pretty much up for anything as well."

"What? Are you," Sara likewise lowered her voice to a whisper, "having sex with your employee?"

Ash plucked a tomato slice out of his sandwich and popped it in his mouth.

"Ash, forget sex. Can we just be friends?"

"Okay. But if you ever need your behind kissed, I'm your man."

Sara hesitated. Ash was a great kisser. What would it be like with two men? Her prudishness was slinking away to the corner where it belonged.

"Besides, Gimpy isn't your type," Ash added.

"I think he might be my soulmate. It's as if no time has passed since we were together before. We just fell back into place."

"Didn't he dump you for a snowboard?"

"In a way, yes. But he came back to me."

"Because he broke his leg darling."

"You're just jealous Ash."

"Of course I'm jealous. He doesn't deserve you. Besides, he's not your soulmate."

"Is too."

"Is not. You were contemplating shagging me just a minute ago."

"Was not."

"Were too. And if Gimpy is your soulmate, you wouldn't think that way."

"I was not contemplating shagging you," Sara lied.

"What do you have in common?" he asked her.

"Fantastic sex."

They both heard the gasps in the gardening aisle.

"The foursome is sounding better and better. Good sex is transitory, love. What then?"

"When's the last time you had good sex?" she asked Ash.

"Last night, with Rosy Palm. She was smashing."

"Real sex."

Ash shifted in his seat. Sara noticed Maddy peep around a bookcase then disappear again.

Sara glanced at the gardening aisle. One Miss Wilson was talking on a cell phone. The other Miss Wilson was staring at Ash with squinty eyes and pursed lips.

"Stop calling Night Gimpy."

"No," Ash said firmly. "This is my store."

After consideration he added, "And what kind of name is Night anyway? Is his last name Night too?"

Sara took a while to make sense of that.

The smile suddenly widened on Ash's face. He was staring over her shoulder. She turned around and saw Andi.

Busted

"Andi, shouldn't you be at T-Squared?" Sara asked her.

"I quit," she told Sara, as she set down the Chinese takeout she had brought for lunch. "Seems like you beat me in everything."

"Andi—"

"It's okay Sara. I've been seeing a life coach. I came here to tell Ash the truth, and I'm glad you're here too."

Ash suddenly looked like a little boy trying to sit still for his mother.

"Ash, I like you. Okay, I'm . . . in love with you. All the guys I talked to and dated were in part a way to avoid my attraction to you. I thought Bryan was my way out, but . . . "

Ash was frozen.

"Sara, you were right about Bryan. Ash, I wanted to be honest with you before I move out of state to start over."

"But," Ash seemed to want to say something, perhaps the ménage à trois offer.

Sara did not know what to say. She was thinking:

1. Andi was too honest.
2. Andi was too good.
3. Andi was too melodramatic.
4. Andi must have cashed in her 401k too.

Ash looked just like a little boy who had raided the cookie jar and thought if he moved a muscle, he would be caught.

Andi stared at Ash with a lovelorn, pleading expression.

Sara turned and saw the Misses Wilson approaching.

"Thou shalt not commit adultery!" said Ethel.

Ash finally moved and gaped at the Misses Wilson as though they were insane.

"You can't have both girls," said Hazel. "We heard everything."

"That's right," Ethel went on, "you can't have this one here, and that one too. It's sinning and Jesus died for your sins, boy."

"I see," Andi said in a small voice.

"No you don't Andi," Sara said quickly, "They're talking about the ménage à trois."

Oops. Sara realized she'd just muddled things further.

Andi seemed to be putting things together in her mind as she looked at Sara, then Ash.

"It's not what you're thinking," Sara told her.

Ash was trying to speak, but only ended up looking like a fish out of water.

"Thank you for your friendship," Andi told them nobly. "Good-bye." She turned and walked toward the door.

Ash finally managed to say, "Wait!"

"The Lord giveth and the Lord taketh away!" said Hazel.

"Young lady," Ethel said to Sara, "we love Mister Ash. Jesus loves him, too. But he is a sinner."

"Bloody hell!" Ash ejaculated.

"It's for your own good, Mister Ash. Your own good."

"Come to church on Sunday," Ethel told him. "The good Lord will wash away your sins."

"I need a drink," Ash said and plopped back down in his chair. "Ladies," he said to the Misses Wilson, "we British blokes follow the example of Henry the Eighth and make up our own commandments. Now, piss off."

The plan accelerates

Sara was looking online at a very large bank balance.

Her 401k was now in her hands. What did melodramatic love triangles matter next to this riveting piece of news?

PopTrends was taking off. Sara saw no reason why she shouldn't spend thousands of dollars on liposuction.

She just had one persistent twinge of anxiety, aside from the warnings of intense—though hopefully short-lived—post surgical pain: Night. Sara did not feel comfortable telling Night about the lipo.

There was nothing for it. Sara did not think lipo was something she could hide from him. For one thing, Dr. Karen warned her that she would be wearing a compression garment for weeks.

Apparently, her skin would be hanging off her with no fat to attach to, and would need time to get its hooks into muscle.

Sex in a compression garment did not sound sexy—or even possible.

On the other hand, Night was into any and all sexual positions, so he might find the challenge attractive.

When Sara looked at the photo of the compression garment, she seriously doubted this positive view of things.

She went ahead and scheduled the lipo with Dr. Karen, and an EKG. No surgery was done until the heart was deemed normal.

Sara was dubious about her heart being normal, since it was ninety percent scar tissue.

She decided to tackle the problem of Night immediately, and as soon as he got home from the climbing gym, Sara brought up her doctor appointment for the EKG.

"Are you, like, sick or something?"

"No, not at all. I'm going to have elective surgery," Sara hedged.

Night looked shell-shocked. "Who on Earth would do that?"

"Well, me apparently. It's . . . liposuction."

Night took this in. Sara could see his brain working it out. "You mean, liposuction?"

Sara rolled her eyes.

"You're going to have fat sucked out? Of where?"

"My thighs." Sara suddenly felt vulnerable. She did not want Night looking at her thighs.

"Why don't you just exercise babe? Listen, a friend in Tahoe—Crystal—lost five pounds fast eating raw foods."

"Crystal?"

"And she won the women's snow-kiting competition."

"I've tried exercising. I've tried dieting."

"Why don't you come to the climbing gym with me? You burn major calories working your core."

"My core's not the problem."

Night unwrapped a chocolate chip nutrition bar and stuffed half of it in his mouth. "Buh, oo cah boo cahohies at way."

"Could you please chew with your mouth closed? Your consonants are dripping down your chin."

Night glared at Sara for a minute, then told her he was going to the health food store for some kefir. Apparently he was in dire need of fermented protein.

Well, thought Sara, that went swimmingly.

Drenched and dreary

Sara wiped sweat off her forehead and continued working her core. Her feet were tucked under the sofa, and she was struggling with sit-up number four.

Five . . .

Six . . .

. . . Sev . . . en . . .

Her cell phone rang and saved her from sit-up number eight. Then the doorbell rang as she checked to see who was calling, and since she was suddenly so busy, she decided seven sit-ups were enough for today.

"This is Sara. Oh, hi Kyle. Um, Friday night?"

Sara peered out the peephole—it was Ash. He was just standing there looking forlorn while rain pelted him. She opened the door and pulled him in.

"Why white? I hate white. It's a surprise? I hate surprises."

Sara rifled through a drawer for a pen. She found a half-dried-up marker. In the meantime, Ash just stood there dripping.

"Got it. Everyone wears white. I hope we won't be serving red wine. Ciao."

Sara suppressed an urge to laugh. Through squinted eyes and pursed lips she regarded Ash.

"Bloody hell," she finally said. "Don't you own an umbrella? I thought umbrellas were mandatory in England. Umbrellas and bicycles."

"You've watched Mary Poppins too many times."

"Oh, so you are speaking. Could you also stop dripping?" Sara threw Ash a kitchen towel. It bounced off his chest and landed in the puddle beneath his feet.

"I'm not speaking. Ever again."

Sara picked up the wet towel and procured a dry one. She removed Ash's coat and dabbed his wettest parts. While blotting his dripping head, she noted with irritation that his wavy hair looked just as good wet as it did dry.

"Come and sit down. I'll make you some tea."

"I'm not drinking tea ever again," said Ash, while he suffered himself to be ensconced on the sofa.

"Ash, I believe I have discovered your dirty little secret—you're a closet drama queen."

"Quite right. I had to come to the States so I could blend in with all the exaggerated egos here."

Sara boiled water and brought Ash a cup of Earl Grey.

"Ash, what's up?"

"My temperature." He grabbed Sara's hand and placed it on his forehead. "Do I have a fever?"

"Are we talking about Andi here?"

"I'm never talking again. I've fired the Misses Wilson as my resident crazies by the way, and hired myself."

"Well, I'm glad. Now, back to Andi."

Ash managed to look even more forlorn.

Sara rolled her eyes to the ceiling and prayed to Cupid for help.

"Tell me what's wrong or I'll never bring you donuts again," she told him.

"If you only knew. My life is beastly. Everybody hates me."

"Who hates you?"

"Oh, just my parents, poor people, book haters, Andi, to name a few."

"Andi doesn't hate you," Sara told him, "she loves you. Or don't you remember that part?"

"Well . . . "

"Ash. I'm a woman—"

"I had noticed," Ash said, breaking into a wicked grin. "I don't normally kiss men. However . . . "

"I thought you loved Andi."

"I never said that. But why did she go? I only have five friends, if you count the Misses Wilson, and now you can't since I fired them."

"Would you like to marry Andi?"

"Marry!"

"Marry."

"Marry, as in marriage? No can do."

"As in, until death do us part. However, we all know that divorce is a painful but sometimes necessary option. That sort of marry. And why can't you do it?"

Ash sipped his Earl Grey and said, "We British blokes prefer complex entanglements over marriage. It's simpler."

The door opened and Night came in with a huge box containing a Thigh Blaster. The photo on the side showed an anorexic twenty-year-old Hollywood bimbo squeezing a spring-loaded contraption between her tanned and toned really skinny thighs.

Sara was torn between hating him for the Thigh Blaster and loving him for his wet and wild rain-drenched look coupled with the rain-fresh aromatic cloud he brought in with him (which oddly she hadn't noticed when Ash came in).

"Hey babe. Look at what I got for you. You'll love it. Hey Ash, how's it goin' man?"

"Ducky," Ash replied flatly.

Night handed Sara a tiny plastic cup with a lid. "Got you a shot of wheatgrass, too. Sorry Ash, I didn't know you would be here."

"How about a shot of Jack as a consolation prize? That'd be brilliant."

"I'll join you Ash," Sara said after slamming down the wheatgrass. It was the only way she could stand it—by opening her throat as wide as possible and throwing the whole lot down at once.

She looked sideways at Ash, who was staring at her. She knew what he was thinking: Why was she drinking wheatgrass just to please Gimpy?

"How about you Gim—Night? Shot of Jack?"

"Sure," he said, throwing himself on the sofa and turning on a video game called Xtreme. He then selected Xtreme skateboarding, and threw Ash a controller.

Ash turned it slowly, trying to find the top.

"Ash owns a bookstore and reads Jane Austen. He doesn't do video games," Sara told Night as she put three shot glasses on the coffee table.

"Piss off," Ash said while fumbling with the knobs and buttons. "I can play video games. This little bugger makes the car go, right?"

"Grinding on skateboards, dude. We can race cars later. *Okole maluna*! That's Hawaiian for bottoms up."

"Long live the queen," said Ash.

"*Kanpai*," said Sara, recalling fond times with Gary—the prick.

Sara took the empty glasses back to the kitchen wondering how many calories were in one shot of Jack. She looked at the Thigh Blaster box. It looked back.

"Stop staring and get to work on your thighs," the box said. "Or are you going to wait until you're too old to do anything about your enormous deposits of cottage cheese?"

"I hate you," Sara hissed to the box.

Night and Ash both looked over at Sara, as their respective skateboarders crashed on a sidewalk.

"What?" Sara said with a wooden smile. "Not you. I was just thinking about . . . the IRS."

To the box she hissed, "I'm getting lipo, bitch."

"You people came to this country to get away from taxation without representation," said Ash. "Why don't you fire the bloody bastards? We like paying the greater portion of our hard-earned wages to a corrupt monarchy in England."

"You don't live in England, Ash."

"A bloody good thing, too—my ego's too big for a small European country."

"No place like America for big fat egos and wallets," said Night.

Sara decided on a second round of shots. She glared at the box on her way to the kitchen. On the way back into the living room, she stuck her tongue out at it.

Yes, she thought defensively, I am a grown woman with mature, reasonable behaviors. It's quite acceptable to dis an obnoxious box.

Night and Ash raised no objections to the second round, although Sara was a bit dubious about the kefir, wheatgrass, and Jack commingling in Night's stomach.

Wear white and suffer the consequences

S ara never wore white. Over thighs such as hers a white dress looked like a tablecloth. In white pants her legs resembled marble pillars.

It had taken her five hours at the mall to find a white outfit. Five hours, and an assortment of cinnamon buns, pretzels, and gooey mall cookies to countermand the stress of shopping for something she did not want.

She finally settled for a crinkly strapless sheath, which, by virtue of the crinkles, hid bulging fat while still looking chic. With high heels and her hair piled high, she found herself wishing the year was 1959. Her padded curves would have been desirable then. But it was the twenty-first century, and desirable women had anorexic boy bodies with double-D breast implants.

Sara reconsidered the idea of breast implants. Perhaps she should add them to the list after all. Between lipo and breast implants, she could make a complete reversal from bottom heavy to top heavy. Besides, she was getting used to pain in the pursuit of beauty.

The dress had cost her more than she'd ever paid for an outfit in her life. But she didn't care. She had her 401k money for courage. She was feeling extra sensitive about her figure after the talk with Night. She wanted to look spectacular for this party.

Night sauntered into the bedroom. He had already dressed and looked as roguish as possible in a white shirt, loose white pants, white tie, bed head hair and white cross-trainers.

"Wow. That's a cool dress," he said. "You look babelicious."

Sara demurred somewhat as Night attempted to cuddle. She had had her hair done and did not want to mess it up. She also felt a bit irritated at his nonstop dude lingo.

However, he kissed her and Night's kisses were rated nine-point-nine-and-three-quarters. The room heated up immediately.

Sara looked at her bedside clock.

"We'll have to continue this later," she told Night. "Time to go."

Night scoured Sara's crinkly dress. "I like the way this feels. Let's be fashionably late."

Sara started to cave in. Then she remembered the Thigh Blaster.

"We're already fashionably late."

"Later then." Night kissed Sara lingeringly and let her go.

On the way to the party Sara's stomach filled up with butterflies whenever she thought of Kyle. Any communications she had had with him lately had been strained and strictly about business.

Well, Kyle was a player and dated the likes of Ever. He was just like all other men who fall for the supermodel version of female: blonde, skinny, enhanced, and barely out of puberty (at least mentally).

Which brought Sara back to thinking about breast implants. Which turned her thoughts back to Night: why did he buy the thigh-blaster and who was Crystal?

The butterflies multiplied.

Just take the thigh-blaster at face value, the little angel on Sara's left shoulder said. No, Night thinks you're fat and cottage cheesy, the little devil on Sara's right shoulder said.

He loves you, and is attracted to you, and came back from the Himalayas to be with you, the little angel on Sara's left shoulder said. No, he left you for the Himalayas and came back to California to be with Crystal, the little devil on Sara's right shoulder said.

*

Shut up already!

*

Sara had a feeling this shindig was going to suck.

Kyle's surprise

Night was a born socializer. His laid-back surfer dude persona might be outdated, but the rogue element was universally attractive. Sara marveled at the ease with which he mingled. Her current conversation with Sandy Moore of Moore Is Less, a weight loss clinic, was boring enough to allow for peripheral tabs on his conquests. She considered that he might be a sales asset to the biz.

"Corn-fed beef is to be avoided at all costs," Ms. Moore told Sara. "The poor cows are overfed to bring them to slaughter quicker, then they pass on their fat cell memories to us when we eat them."

Sara looked at her little plate of hors d'oeuvres, scanning for cow.

"And refined white sugar is the scourge of the civilized world. Can you imagine eating donuts for breakfast?"

Sara smiled, glad the question was rhetorical. "It's about lifestyle," Sara said, quoting her own copy from the ad she was writing. "A fundamental change in thinking."

"Yes. Exactly. Take you for instance. What don't you like about yourself, your appearance?"

Sara hesitated. Did she want to expose that to someone who thought white sugar was the scourge of the civilized world? No.

Avoiding the truth, Sara said, "Nothing. Well . . . except my age. I'd like to shave a few years off."

"Wouldn't we all," Ms. Moore said with arched eyebrows. "What about your hips? Most women want thinner hips and thighs."

"Well," Sara began, trying not to glare indignantly at Ms. Moore. Then, the music got louder, and changed from classical to techno.

Someone on a microphone was announcing, "White is right tonight!"

Sara saw Jason Blane, a clothing designer, standing on a runway, announcing his new summer white-gold line. His spiked hair was so bleached he resembled Billy Idol from the eighties.

" . . . hot white flames of desire ladies and gentlemen. Golden delicious and white up your alley. Check it out!"

Sara cringed at Jason's bad play on words as the crowd was riveted to the runway. The runway Kyle had apparently had installed for tonight's gala. Sara had seen it of course, and speculated that a fashion show of some kind might be pending. But as she loathed skinny models and fashions which only looked good on them, she had avoided acknowledging its presence as long as possible.

But her attention was inexorably drawn to the parade of super-skinny super-gorgeous supermodels wearing Jason's designs, and Ever was in the lead wearing . . . nothing?

Ever's thong bikini was so small, so nonexistent, she looked naked. When she bounced her way down the runway no other part of her bounced but her implants. Sara was sure she was going to vomit right there and then, all over her white dress.

"Cool," Night said behind her. He had rested his hand on her shoulder, but when Sara turned to look at him, his eyes were lit up like Hummer headlights. All the men were cheering, including Night, and dancing to the techno. Sara wondered why the men were not too shy to dance to this, when she guessed—rightly so—that they never wanted to dance with their partners on a dance floor until they were drunk. Hateful.

On the other hand, Sara noticed that many of the women had frozen smiles, or outright scowls of disapproval. This cheered her up considerably.

Skinny model after skinny model paraded Jason's line of clothing, made apparently exclusively for twenty-something, size-one, five-foot-tenners with breast implants. Hateful.

Sara saw Kyle in the crowd, beebopping to the music with the other teenaged boys, his face aglow. Then she saw him wink at Ever.

That's when Sara made her way through the back door to the paved alley, where the ostracized smokers were gathered like a pack of despicable, hunched rodents.

She basked in the risen crescent moon, and repeated her mantra to de-stress:

"Liposuction, liposuction, liposuction . . . "

She didn't care what Night thought about it, she was sucking the cottage cheese out of her thighs, like it or not. Then she was going to get veneers. Then she was going to get breast implants. When all of that was done, it would be time for a facelift.

"Sara."

Sara opened her eyes and turned around. It was Kyle. She was surprised he could tear himself away from the fashion show long enough to speak to his entire creative team (her).

"Oh hi Kyle. Why didn't you tell me we were having a pornographic fashion show?"

"We haven't been talking much lately," he told her.

"How's Ever? She looks a little cold in that mouse-thong."

"She's hot actually, don't you think?"

Sara stared at him through slits-for-eyes.

"Stop it Sara. You know why Ever's in the picture. Without her father, our little operation starts over. Do you really think I care about her?"

"Why should I care? I just don't like this kind of male-oriented 60's Playboy Club crap. I hope you didn't lose Ms. Moore's patronage because of it."

"Some of the models are her clients."

"Do you think any women in there are going to buy those bathing suits?"

"That's not the point Sara."

"Well I suppose it's better than a fashion show featuring adult diapers."

Kyle's lips pursed. He was trying not to smile.

"Why don't you like Ever?" he asked her.

Sara contemplated her answer while listening to the muffled sounds of techno thumping through the steel door.

Gorgeous.

Skinny.

Rich.

Spoiled.

Then the music stopped and she looked at Kyle. She felt his eyes burning holes into her soul. She could not look away. His eyes were trying to tell her something.

Just then the door opened and a group of fresh smokers emerged from the fashion show. Night also came out, looking for Sara.

"Hey babe," Night said when he saw Sara. "How's it goin' man," he said to Kyle clapping a handshake on him.

"It's going well," Kyle said flatly Sara thought. "Excuse me, I've got to get back in and babysit the guests."

"Babe," Night said as he drew her to him. "I've been offered a job. Isn't that cool?"

"By whom?"

"Sandy. Sandy Moore that is. She needs an assistant, and I'm her man."

"That's great." Sara was relieved. She wasn't sure when Night was going to get a job with his leg broken. Having him around twenty-four-seven was seriously affecting her work-at-home gig. And she did not want to go into the office with the strained relationship currently boiling between her and Kyle.

"And I've been thinking. As soon as my leg is better, let's go to Hawaii."

"Well," Sara said remembering how much Night liked all play and no work, "what about your new job?"

"Great waves there babe. I'll teach you to surf."

"I don't know," Sara told him, "we're just getting PopTrends off the ground. Maybe next year."

"I have a good reason," Night said while pulling her to him. "We gel, ya know. It's as if no time has passed since we were together before. We fit. We're soulmates, babe. I want us to get married."

PART IX
Turning forty won't be so bad now . . .

Confused instead of happy

S ara was chewing her index fingernail off in little typewriter-row bites. When it was done, she spat the nail out . . .

*

Zzzzzzzip bang!

*

. . . and she started the typewriter action on her middle fingernail. In this way, working through her fingernails, she drove to Bookaholic to talk to Ash.

She was rehearsing what she was going to say to Ash while negotiating turns with one hand and stopping obediently at every red light.

"Ash, guess what? Gimpy, I mean Night, wants to get married. Well, not really married as such, but say our vows to each other on the beach with our feet in the ocean. He knows a woman in Hawaii who marries people, a new-age minister of sorts, who also does palm-reading by the way—I wonder if she knows Celestara—because who really needs a piece of paper, and wouldn't it be beautiful, and I'm going to be forty so . . . "

Sara imagined Ash saying, "Bloody hell!"

"But Ash, just because you don't like Gimp—I mean Night, doesn't mean he's not good for me. He's my soulmate."

"Is not!"

"Is too!"

"Is not!"

"Bloody hell Ash! It's my life!"

And so on, until she arrived at the bookstore.

The sign said closed, but Sara went in anyway as the door was open.

She heard scuffling and something akin to grunting in the aisles and thought it must be the Misses Wilson. She did not see Ash, but soon Maddy emerged from the cookbook aisle looking disheveled, smoothing her black hair, and looking more like a vampire than ever.

Sara wondered if she'd been sucking Ash's blood.

Maddy was startled when she saw Sara. Then Ash emerged from the same aisle and Sara stared at him with slits-for-eyes.

His anime hair was sticking out in all directions, and he still looked dashing.

"Darling, why are you biting your nails?"

"Hi Sara," Maddy said as though she'd been caught doing something questionable, which she had.

"Hi Maddy." To Ash she said, "Have you got a minute?"

"Well darling, I thought the signed said closed, but for you," Ask winked, "it's always open."

"I'm heading home," said Maddy. "Goodnight," she said to them both.

"Goodnight," from Sara.

"Nighty-night," from Ash.

When the door closed, Sara turned her slits-for-eyes on Ash.

"What?" he whined.

"You know what."

Ash plunked down at his desk and drew out a bottle of Jack and two shot glasses of dubious cleanliness.

"Stop looking at me like that," he whined some more while pouring. "If you knew everything you'd be queen."

"What does that mean?" Sara whined back at him.

"It means, oh bloody hell, Maddy is my flippin' wife. There." And he downed a shot, then poured another.

Sara just stared. Then she stared some more. Then she said, "Pour me one."

Ash handed her the full shot glass and poured another for himself.

Sara sat down and stared some more. Ash stared with her.

They seemed to be at a stupefying impasse while Sara tried to process this information by going over their entire history together as friends.

Finally Sara mused, "And I thought you hired Maddy because she was the only applicant with an British accent."

"Okay love. If you must know all the sordid details . . . "

"I must," Sara said.

"My dear Uncle Edmund, dear dear Uncle Edmund, dear dear dear—"

"Get on with it Ash."

"This was the deal. Wed Madeleine Sunderland, daughter of Sir Colin Sunderland, friend of dear Sir Uncle Edmund, unite the two illustrious families, or, no money."

"You sold out to Uncle Edmund?"

"Well I didn't want to go to work for bloody sake!"

"What about Maddy? She just went along with it?"

"She didn't have much of a choice either. You don't know these British families—they think they're all kings and queens, and their children are the pawns."

"Maybe, but it's better than being one of the peasants."

"Anyway, Maddy wanted to come to the states to get away from all that, as I did. So we made a deal. We'd be married in name only. And once we got here, we'd live separate lives and go our own ways."

"What was that in the cookbook aisle then?"

"That? Just a little slap and tickle. Conjugal rights and all that. What? She wanted it too."

"Why on Earth didn't you tell me Ash?"

"There was no reason to," he told her. "We're not *really* married. Just married on paper."

Sara mused over this while thoughts chased tail in her head. Poor Ash . . . well, that wasn't accurate. He certainly was not poor, thanks to dear Uncle Edmund.

"Is that why you never take women seriously, because you can't? Like Andi?"

Ash shrugged. Ash smirked.

"No it's not," Sara realized with increasing irritation. "This actually works in your favor doesn't it? It gives you an excuse not to commit."

"So what if it does? It's not true anyway. I'm an honorable man."

All Sara said was, "Cookbook aisle."

"Bollocks," Ash said and poured another shot.

"How could you be so mad at Bryan for having a wife? Oh, okay, I get it. That's WHY you were mad at him. Because you—"

"Sara," he said with a dangerous gleam in his eye, "we British blokes do not like being psychoanalyzed."

Sara remembered that Ash really was her best friend. She should be supporting him, but what she wanted to do was fix him.

"Okay Ash, what if you—"

"Forget it Sara. It is what it is. After dear Uncle Edmund drops dead, Maddy and I will get divorced and split the pile. That is, if the will doesn't say we can't."

"I wish you had told me," Sara admitted. "But, oh well. Speaking of marriage . . . "

Ash looked up and the cogs in his brain were turning, possibly greased by the Jack.

"Gimpy?" he asked.

"Yes."

"Gimpy wants to get married?"

Sara prevaricated, "Well, not married as such."

"You mean, like my marriage? Does he have a knighted rich uncle too?"

"I mean," Sara told him, "he wants to exchange vows, but not in the traditional way. On the beach, with a friend of a friend of his who does 'commitment ceremonies.'" Sara left out the palm-reading part. "It's romantic really. And who wants a wedding that appeases everyone but the bride and groom?"

"Commitment ceremony? I'm a guy Sara. Trust me, this would not be a commitment ceremony. If he was truly committed he would go for the whole biscuit."

"He's not conventional Ash. I like that about him."

"What beach?"

"Hawaii, not sure which island."

Ash peered at Sara, then said, "Who am I to judge? I'm the tosser who sold out to dear Uncle Edmund. When's the wedding, or rather, the ceremony?"

"Don't know yet. I haven't exactly agreed."

Sara was biting her nicely plumped bottom lip.

Sara has an epiphany

"Yikes," Sara said. "These handholds are too far away."

"Lunge," Night told her.

Sara lunged. After all, she was only four feet off the floor, strapped into a harness and hanging from ropes on belay.

She grabbed the handhold, which looked like a blob of petrified gorilla poop, and stepped over to another blob of petrified gorilla poop. Thankfully, until Night's leg was healed, they would climb at the gym only, and not out on some vertical rock cliff where spiders or snakes might be lurking in the crevices.

"You're doing great, babe," Night said. And Sara scurried up a few more feet. Then she repelled down—her favorite part—which required no muscle tone or particular skill.

On the way home they stopped and got a shot of wheat grass. Sara felt so healthy, and so fit, she almost contemplated canceling her liposuction.

But not quite.

While Sara was showering, Night slipped in. He washed her back with the loofah, and reached around to soap up her breasts with his hands. By this time, Sara felt something rising, stiff and eager, between her thighs.

After a bit of shower shagging, she shut the water off, and they made their way to the bed, limping and dripping.

Sara had to admire Night for his athletic ability. His broken leg, although it was almost done healing, did not hamper him in the least.

Goose bumpy, wet, hot and cold, they scoured the bed with passion. Sara thought sadly of George, who had seen no action since Night had arrived. Not for long however, since Night was coaxing her into a lovely position on their sides, where their legs were entwined love vines.

Afterwards, Sara lay panting on Night's nicely muscled shoulder. She started to say something, but realized he was twitching. He had fallen asleep in seconds. Sara envied this ability to let go. She, on the other hand, being a certified worrywart, needed complex strategies in order to fall asleep, let alone take a nap.

She got up and pulled on pajama bottoms and a t-shirt—her official work uniform—and went to her computer.

She checked her personal ad messages. A few new guys were interested. She deleted them and thought that it was about time she stopped looking for her soulmate now that she was with her soulmate.

Apparently White Cloud was on the Arizona leg of his book tour.

She deleted her weekly bulk email from Dave:

"ur so sexy. i luv smart womin. do u hav a webcam?"

One from Bryan:

"Just thought I'd say hey. B."

Relentless. Sara couldn't help but relive the sofa pounding.

"Jeez," she mumbled to herself, "what's wrong with me?" She had just been gloriously shagged by the love of her life, and she was thinking about sex with Bryan.

After talking to Ash about his unfortunate marriage, she was feeling less judgmental of Bryan. One should not judge until one has walked a mile in another's moccasins, or something to that effect.

"Bollocks," Sara admonished herself again. She was actually contemplating another sofa pounding on the sly. "I'm the Viking slut all over again! I'm never satisfied!"

Suddenly Sara got a rush of goose bumps. She thought of Night's devil-may-care athleticism. The way he just went off for a jaunt in the Himalayas, as the Vikings used to do in their ships, leaving the poor Viking women home alone (and there were no dildos then, but perhaps they grew cucumbers).

What if . . .

What if Night was the Viking she had cheated on in her past life? What if that was why Night was shying away from a real wedding? What if this was her chance to make it up to him?

What if this was her chance to balance her karmic debt? (She'd heard that phrase before, and it seemed fitting now.)

She knew what she had to do. She had to see Celestara again.

Hurricane Sara

W ell, Celestara was booked four months out. However, she did do phone consultations for her return clients, and she had an open slot today. Her "love donation" of a suggested one-fifty—that's one hundred and fifty—could be sent via PayPal.

Sara thought, Andi and Ash paid that much for my birthday present?

And she thought, Love donation . . . that's a great way to avoid paying taxes. Too bad I can't figure out a way for PopTrends to do that.

She made the online payment to Celestara and confirmed the phone appointment.

A text message came through from Andi.

> Are you there?

Sara had to think about that.

> Yeah. What's up?

> Sorry for my emotional outburst. Still here.

Right, thought Sara. What a drama queen.

> Wanna have lunch?

Busy today.

> Tomorrow?

> Pretty please?

Okay. How about the sandwich shop?

> Noon?

One.

> Great. One.

Sara sighed and rolled her eyes to heaven. She simply did not have time for Andi's romantic issues. She was juggling a new business, a confusing business partner, looming elective surgery, and a Viking come home to roost.

Throw in PMS, and we have a shit storm. The shit storm was in Sara's head at the moment. She was thinking:

Why on Earth would Kyle imagine I could *like* Ever?

And,

Does Andi want me to intervene on her behalf with Ash or Bryan? Wait till she finds out Ash has a wife, too.

And,

Marriage! To Night! Oh wait, not really marriage. Commitment ceremony. What the hell is that, really?

And,

I can't wait until my thighs are thin. I hope they give me good pain medication.

And,

I've got a zillion spots to write. Crap! I can't think!

And,

Who's going to pay for a trip to Hawaii?

And so on.

By the time Sara made the call to Celestara, the shit storm had turned into a full-fledged hurricane. Hurricane Sara.

Sara's stomach was in knots while Celestara made the necessary invocations, lighting of candles, and other vital introductions for a session with the Beyond.

So, now what?

"Your twin flame is very near, but shying away from you now."

"Twin flame? I was thinking soulmate. What's a twin flame?"

"You may have many soulmates," Celestara told Sara, "but the twin flame is your true mate, the other half of yourself. Your twin flame is also a soulmate."

Sara considered the hot sex she always had with Night, and thought "twin flame" was certainly appropriate.

Twin flame, soulmate, jeez, Sara thought, the karma overlords don't make this easy.

"Your twin flame is afraid . . . of being hurt . . . he is the one—"

"The Viking I cheated on in a past life?" Sara interjected.

"Yes."

"I knew it!"

"He is . . . waiting, for a sign from you."

"Yeah. He did ask me something."

"Hmmmm . . . " Celestara listened to The Twelve while Sara waited with bated breath for cosmic counsel.

"My guides are telling me that if you don't get it right this time, you will be separated again for a long time. A very long time. You will have to work out your karma on your own, possibly for many more lifetimes."

Sara's heart sank. She was already being tempted by the likes of Bryan.

"But, there's one thing I don't understand. You told me that my soulmate, or I guess now it's my twin flame, wouldn't show up until I loved myself."

"He's always been here. Loving yourself is part of the pattern. It's all interwoven. Your twin flame will *help* you, but he can't do it *for* you."

Sara was certain of one thing: she was certain of nothing. If she didn't get it right with Night, would she have to spend the rest of her life—and how many more lifetimes—alone and miserable?

She was more confused than ever.

The next day at lunch, Sara told Andi about Night's "proposal" and Celestara's warning.

"Your twin flame," Andi breathed with feeling. "You're so lucky!"

"Lucky? How do you figure that? I'm with my twin flame, soulmate, whatever, and I still have fantasies about other men. I'm the Viking slut all over again. And I have the thighs to prove it."

"Who do you have fantasies about?"

"Whom," Sara said to gain time.

"Whom, then."

Sara fiddled with her napkin. "Well, you know, movie stars."

"Movie stars don't count."

"I'm a wreck. I don't know what to do."

"It's easy Sara. Marry him."

"It's not really marriage."

"Whatever it is, do it. He's the one for you. You love him don't you?"

"What is love anyway? I'll tell you this: if sex were love, I'd be all over this. But it's more than that. I've always been head-over-heels for Night. But that was when I couldn't have him. Now that I can . . . but can I? He doesn't really want marriage because he doesn't trust the Viking slut. See? I'm a babbling idiot!"

Sara noticed that Andi was looking forlorn. Not that that was unusual; Andi was always forlorn about something just for the poetic effect. Sara tore herself away from her own drama and reluctantly asked about Andi's drama.

"It's just that," Andi told her, "you know, it's . . . "

"Well, that was informative. Now would you try to speak in complete sentences?"

"Okay. I fall in love with everybody. Ash, Bryan, Hans . . . I'm even a little bit in love with you."

Sara was flattered, but definitely not interested.

"Andi, you're just a loving person. That's all. But what is the problem?"

"No one loves me back."

"They all love you back, Andi. The problem, I think, is what you expect that love to be."

. . . The problem . . . is what you expect that love to be.

It was as though her voice had been filtered through an echo chamber.

Something clicked. Something fell into place.

Sara knew what to do about Night.

Sara rejects the box

"Well, ma'am—"

"Don't call me ma'am," Sara told the airhead at Sports Style return counter. "Do I look like a ma'am?"

The airhead at the return counter did not know how to answer that. So he said, "Are you sure you want to return this . . . miss? Was there something wrong with it?"

The airhead was trying not to look at Sara's thighs.

"Look. I don't want this skinny bitch," Sara plunked the box over and pointed to the Hollywood babe squeezing the Thigh Blaster, "showing me how to sweat blood with this torture device when she probably had her rich husband who by the way is in midlife crisis pay for her liposuction for which she traded sexual favors."

All the airhead heard was a run-on sentence and "sexual favors."

"Um . . ."

Sara took pity on the airhead. "How about giving me a store credit since I don't have the receipt? Can you do that?"

"Sure, yes." The airhead took the box and Sara breathed a sigh of relief. She was happy not to have to deal with that box anymore.

She left the store with a plastic store credit card, which she would give to Night.

For some strange reason, getting rid of that box made Sara's creativity flow. She spent the latter part of the day finishing several spots she had been struggling over.

Sara didn't even hear Night come in from work, until she noticed the shower was running. She thought fleetingly of getting in it with him, but decided it was actually yummier to keep writing.

Which did strike her as odd. But perhaps, she mused, I'm finally growing up. Just in time to decay and decline, alas.

Sara was pecking away happily when Night came into her office. "I'm starved," he said.

"Me too. How was work today?"

"Great. How about lentils and rice? Do we have any broccoli?"

"Cake and ice cream sounds better." Sara smiled at him and her heart thunked when he gave her a roguish half-smile. He was just so dang cute.

"Night," she said. "Here's the thing. I do love you. I do want to say yes to your 'proposal.' But, I need you to accept me for who I am."

"I do, babe."

Instead of saying, What about the Thigh Blaster? Sara said, "I mean, if I want liposuction, it should be okay with you. It doesn't mean I won't exercise," Sara felt like she should be crossing her fingers behind her back, "it means, don't expect me to be something I'm not."

Night knelt down in front of Sara. "Okay babe. I was just trying to help, my way. Raw food diets—"

"Night, do you love me the way I am, now?"

"Of course."

"And lipo is okay with you?"

"If it's really what you want, yeah."

"I've been thinking about this commitment thing. I expect real commitment to mean marriage. I'm willing to let go of that expectation."

"You mean, you'll marry me?"

"It's not marriage."

"It is to me. I don't need a piece of paper from some government office."

"Okay then, yes."

Night smiled a happy, roguish, crooked smile and Sara's heart thunked again.

She breathed a sigh of relief. This was the right thing to do. She loved Night; she wanted to cancel her Viking slut karmic debt; she was almost forty and wouldn't have to be "single" anymore.

This was the right thing to do. But, who was going to pay for a trip to Hawaii?

A wedding to plan

S ara was looking at her calendar. There were two weddings coming up: hers, and Greg's. She was just going to go ahead and call her commitment vows to Night a wedding. It was simpler.

A Hawaii wedding simplified things. Just she and Night would go. They would come back "married" and no one would ask embarrassing questions such as:

1. What's a commitment ceremony?
2. What if you have kids? Oh, but how old are you anyway?
3. If he dies, do you inherit his estate?

Not that Night had an estate, although Sara really didn't know. The whole time Sara had known Night, he had worked to live, and skipped from one job to the next to pay for his adventures.

The little devil on Sara's right shoulder said, And why, at your age, are you with a guy who can't keep a job? Because, said the little angel on Sara's left shoulder, he's your soulmate, twin flame, whatever.

"Okay, shut up already!" Sara said brushing off her shoulders.

"Nobody likes advice, particularly from imaginary archetypes that look like Disney characters."

The glitch was this: Unless PopTrends started paying her more now, Sara was going to have to make a decision between liposuction and Hawaii.

Liposuction was the Holy Grail, but Hawaii was karmic debt paid, cash on the barrelhead.

Liposuction . . . karmic debt . . . bloody hell!

Of course, they could "commit" without going to Hawaii and stand in a pool maybe, or a mud puddle. But then her friends would attend and she would have to answer those embarrassing questions.

*

Aarrrrgh!

*

Sara sighed and knew that liposuction would have to be postponed. She just hoped to have her thighs done before her aging flesh began to wrinkle and drape over her knees. However, she was quite sure that during the liposuction surgery, they could hike up the sag and sew it in place. She would ask Dr. Karen.

She wouldn't have to postpone it for long. Night was working, and PopTrends was taking off. She would start getting commissions. In the meantime, she had found her soulmate—she was just going to go ahead and call her twin flame a soulmate, it was simpler—and she was pubic hair-free below the bikini line, just in time to lounge on a beach in Hawaii.

On another positive note, Sara considered with some glee showing up at Greg and Brittney's boring, conventional wedding with her fiancé, Night: roguish, cute, charming, and devoted. She considered showing up and casually rubbing her new business with Kyle in Brittney's face. She was definitely going to RSVP the invitation.

PART X
The best laid plans of mice and men (and women) often go awry

Kyle and the sunbeams

Humanity has trodden a long and winding road, so to speak, and doesn't seem any closer to being an evolved species. The question begs to be asked: Will humans ever stop being afraid of rejection and confess the truth about their feelings to other humans pretending that they don't care either?

Kyle sat at his office desk staring into the middle distance. Although there were billions of dust particles happily swimming in the sunbeams streaming through the window, and although the window presented a nice view of the zeroscaped courtyard, he saw none of that.

He saw Sara's face. Sara of the cottage cheese thighs. Sara of the witty comebacks. Sara of the intense gaze and impish smile. Sara, who was dating a rogue and loving it apparently.

Kyle was many things but not a rogue. He was spoiled by affluent and indulgent parents, used to getting his way, smart and business-savvy, able to reach long-term goals in a single leap, not bad-looking, well muscled, kind—well usually—but he was not a rogue.

Kyle considered his goals. He considered his careful planning.

The plan was: Get the business going and prove himself. Make his own fortune. Enjoy the dating pool supply while he was young, virile, and climbing the ladder of success.

But now, there was Sara. Sara of the impish smile.

Kyle seethed into the middle distance.

As Kyle was seething at ignored sunbeams, his office door opened.

Ever peeked around the door and said, "Hey."

"Hey," Kyle parroted while smiling his best smile, which was very good, and greeted his key client's beautiful but shallow daughter.

She walked in and sat on his desk, smiling, glowing, wearing very little very well.

"Daddy says he's got a few people lined up. They're looking for someone to give their money to. What are you doing tonight?"

Working late

Sara let herself into PopTrends' offices. Night was driving her nuts talking about Hawaiian breakers and Kahuna the surf god. She left him exercising his now healed but weak leg while streaming all the surfing videos he could find.

The place was empty. Sara went to her office and settled at her modern desk, in the ergonomic chair. She logged in and opened a file she was working on.

She took a moment to savor the experience. Here she was, in her very own office, in a business with enormous potential, doing work that really blew her skirt up. Everything smelled new. Sara got the same feeling when she bought a new car, except that this was way more exciting. She could almost forget she ever wanted to write espionage novels.

She pulled the High Priestess card out of her purse and set it in front of her silvery gooseneck lamp.

She was both glad and disappointed that Kyle was not around. She would have to tell him about the week in Hawaii. It's not that she thought he would balk at her taking the time off. She just didn't want to tell him.

An offer that can't be refused

The Montezuma Room at the Aztec resort featured a sacrificial pyramid in the middle of its great expanse, laden with late-night gourmet desserts and snacks.

Kyle looked over the faire, and selected a crystal cup of ceviche from a bed of ice. Ever chose a prickly pear mousse and they rejoined her father and his associates—Miriam Kash, Manny Halikowski, and Josie Nguyen—at their table.

"As I was saying," Jack said, "in order to stay on the leading edge of this industry, you've got to diversify. Isn't that right my boy?"

Jack clapped a meaty hand on Kyle's shoulder.

"That's right Mr. Crumb," Kyle said. "Media is expanding on a daily basis. We produce short, interactive videos for short, bored attention spans, capable of being viewed on anything—phones, tablets, laptops, whatever devices come along."

"I've got three cable shows in the gutter right now not pulling their weight," said Miriam. "Can you get me traffic? The turnover is killing me."

"I can get you traffic," said Kyle. "I can hook an audience. You'll have to take it from there."

She said, "I can take it from there. You just bring me the horny housewives and the wannabe chefs."

"Listen kid," Manny said, "are you going public with this thing?"

"No sir, not now. Venture capital only. I want to slip in under the radar, grow quietly at first. But I can offer you a high rate of return. And that, on a sure deal. I know my business. You can count on that."

"I know your parents," said Manny. "I believe you're capable. But the Internet is unpredictable, fickle."

"I disagree, sir. That is, if you know what you're doing, and I do."

Ever slipped a tiny spoonful of mousse between her lips. Manny coughed into his napkin.

Josie sat listening through the conversation but had no questions or comments. Kyle suspected that she was the really big money. He knew better than to schmooze her with Hollywood smiles, flattery, or enthusiastic predictions. So he started throwing out some solid numbers.

That got her attention.

While Kyle laid out the projections, Jack pulled a cigar out and rolled it between his thumb and finger. When an appropriate spot in the conversation presented itself, he asked Kyle to join him on the veranda.

Lighted palm trees, water features, sparkling pools and Aztec sculptures spilled out over expansive grounds. Jack lit up his cigar and told Kyle that he owned ten percent of the Aztec.

Kyle raised his eyebrows.

"Yes, my boy. I've got my hands into many pots. Diversify, remember?"

"You're a smart businessman, Mr. Crumb."

"Jack, please. Had a lot of luck. A lot of breaks. Right place at the right time."

"You're being modest."

Jack lit his cigar and confessed that he was. "It's true though. I did have lucky breaks. But, I'll admit to being a business genius."

Kyle laughed with Jack.

"You've got Nguyen on the edge of her seat ready to open her considerable wallet. You're good."

Kyle met Jack's eyes. "I am. It's a talent of mine. But it's all true. This venture is taking off and will keep right on going."

Jack blew a stream of smoke and rolled his cigar after tapping the ash.

"On my fifth wife, you know. Good woman, not too bright. Great sex."

"Fifth?"

"Fifth. Money can buy just about anything. Let me tell you son, there is nothing like a good woman to come home to. Nothing. Of course, coming home to a woman in a twelve-thousand-square-foot house makes it all the more palatable."

"The house can wait. I've got ladders to climb."

"And you're making a damned good job of it. How are things going with my beautiful daughter?"

"Fine, sir. Ever has been very helpful."

"Helpful, yes. She likes you. Ever is . . . unstable. Impulsive. I'm to blame. Spoiled her rotten."

"Spoiled isn't the worst thing to be. I'm a product of it myself. Parents mean well."

"Yes," Jack agreed. He clapped Kyle on the back and said, "Yes they do. And this parent needs to hand his spoiled daughter off to someone he can trust. It's got to be someone she likes because . . . it's easier that way. She needs a stabilizing influence. She needs someone like you."

Kyle looked at Jack, but didn't say anything.

"Love is overrated. Take my advice. I've been married five times."

"I respect your advice, Jack. I like Ever, but—"

"No buts. I hate that word. There's no hardship involved here my boy. Any man would be happy to hang Ever off his arm. I've got my heart set on this. You want Nguyen? The price is my daughter."

Back at the office

"Yes!"

Kyle let himself into PopTrends' offices and smiled. Sara was here and apparently happy about something.

"Is that you Kyle?" she said from her office.

"Yeah, me."

He walked back and leaned against her doorway.

"Isn't it late to be working?"

"Look who's talking. And who says I'm working? How do you know I'm not trying to hack into the IRS database?"

"That would qualify as work in my opinion. Very good for business."

"I finally came up with a great spot for Gelato Squisito. Fruits, nuts, cocoa beans, and vanilla pods being squeezed and the juices and powders flowing, all backlit and beautiful. The copy will run to sexy, with gorgeous Italians licking their lips. The copy, oh the copy . . . micro romance stories."

"Women buy eighty percent of the ice cream."

"Right. So, we have to find some sexy, irresistible Italian men."

"That's the easy part," Kyle said. "They seem to have dark and handsome down, and tall won't matter on video."

"I feel good about this now, after being stuck on the project. The name—I kept thinking squid-flavored ice cream."

"Get that thought right out of your wonderful head and think, romance."

"I'm on it," Sara said and smiled. Kyle smiled back. There were no sunbeams, but the dust particles were swimming quite giddily in the lamplight.

"Anyway, yes, I'm working late. I love the office. But I love working at home too. Life is good."

"Life is good," parroted Kyle.

"I . . . want to thank you Kyle. I never thought to be actually *happy* at a job. More than happy . . . inspired is a better word."

Kyle grabbed a chair and sat down at Sara's desk. "It's not just a job," he pointed out.

"I know. But just let me say how much I appreciate this opportunity."

"I appreciate your talents, Sara. I'm good at what I do. But so are you. We make a good team."

"My life is so different now. I used to want to write espionage novels. I think because I wanted to escape. Now I want to write—"

"—Romance," Kyle finished for her, and they laughed.

Sara looked at Kyle. She needed to tell him about Hawaii, but still couldn't muster up the courage.

Why would it take courage? asked the little angel on Sara's left shoulder. Because you're only marrying Night to pay off karmic debt, said the little devil on Sara's right shoulder.

Sara brushed off her right shoulder and said, "Lint ball."

Kyle wasn't blinking. It made Sara look away.

"Hey," she said, "have you got anything alcoholic here? We could drink to Gelato Squisito."

"I do. Gifts from well-wishers. Hold on."

Kyle went to his office, and came back with a bottle of cognac.

"French, and very exclusive. Limited run. Twenty-five hundred a bottle, or thereabouts."

"Wow. That's like, two hundred dollars a sip. The bottle is beautiful," Sara said.

"Designed by a famous French artist—can't remember his name. It's crystal."

Sara wasn't sure she liked cognac, but she was fairly certain this would be good.

Kyle opened the bottle and handed it to her.

"What, no brandy snifters?"

"Nope. We'll have to chug it out of the bottle."

The absurdity of this proposition was absolutely delicious.

Sara took a sip. It warmed her tongue, then her throat, and spread tingling all the way through to her fingers and toes.

Damn, Sara thought, there goes two hundred bucks!

She handed the bottle to Kyle. He sipped, closed his eyes, and said, "Not bad."

"Let me try that again," Sara said and retrieved the bottle. "To Gelato Squisito."

This time she could taste it better on her primed tongue and decided it was more than not bad. "This stuff rocks," she told Kyle as she handed the bottle back.

Kyle chuckled and raised it in the air. "To romance," he said.

Sara felt loose and rubbery. She suggested they sit.

"No, not on chairs," she told Kyle. "Let's sit on the floor and lean against the wall. It's more in keeping with chugging out of a twenty-five-hundred-dollar crystal bottle. We'll pretend we're wandering the streets of Paris because someone stole our passports. We bought the cognac for Aunt Margaret back home. But since we're stuck in Paris, we've decided to stare at the Eiffel Tower and drown our sorrows."

"Aunt Margaret has expensive tastes. Is she your aunt or mine?"

"Yours. My aunt's tastes run to crocheted potholders. She gets the spoon that says, Paris, France. That is, if we ever get back."

"And, why did we go to Paris?"

"Why else . . . "

"Romance," they both said and laughed.

Sara felt her insides tingling. The cognac was slowly disappearing.

She continued, "You have a bank account in Switzerland that you didn't think I knew about. However, I'm nosy, and found out but never told you. So, I suggest we just hang out in Paris and live off your squirreled-away money."

"But I was saving that for you," Kyle said, wanting to contribute to the story, "in case I died in a freak accident before the insurance policy matured."

"How nice of you. But without passports, we could be stuck in Paris a long time. You know how slowly the wheels of government grind."

"Well then, to Paris." Kyle drank and passed the bottle. Sara said, "To Paris."

Kyle held her eyes as she drank. "And?" he said.

"And, we find an apartment. It's over a café. The smells of fresh-baked French bread and strong coffee come in the window each morning. We laugh and go out to the balcony, where Francois uses a pole with a hook to lift a basket of bread and two cups of French roast to us. The coffee always spills a little but we don't care."

"We don't care," said Kyle.

"Months go by waiting for our passports. We learn to speak passable French and I wear my hair long and wavy, and you . . . "

Sara rested her head against the wall and turned to look at Kyle. He was watching her with bated breath.

"You stop cutting your hair too. It's getting shaggy and falls in your eyes. You wear your shirts unbuttoned and sketch French girls at the café downstairs in a little journal I bought for you. With your Swiss money of course."

"I can't draw."

"You didn't think you could, but after I bought you the journal and encouraged you with my newly acquired French-girl wiles, your talents flowered. The shaggy hair helped."

"And you?"

"I write a racy novel on an old typewriter I found at a second-hand market. I sell it to an American publisher and it becomes a best-seller."

"We don't have to live off of my squirreled-away money anymore."

"No. And I have my royalties wired to your Swiss bank account. Our Swiss bank account now."

"And our passports?"

"We got those reissued months ago. But we don't want to go back to the states. We're too happy."

"We're too happy."

Sara's head had somehow gotten closer to Kyle's. Their shoulders were touching. His bottom lip was wet, smeared with two-hundred-dollar-a-sip cognac.

"We like Paris," he said. "It's so . . . "

"European . . . sleazy . . . "

"Romantic . . . "

Kyle's bottom lip was wet and Sara was going to taste it. Taste his bottom lip, because it looked so . . . so . . .

She began moving toward Kyle. Kyle began moving toward Sara. The movements were so small they were almost unnoticeable. Almost, but not quite unnoticeable, because the heat in the room was ratcheting up considerably.

Kyle's bottom lip was a couple of inches away. Sara could already feel his lips. They were firm and yielding, aggressive and gentle. He was her French lover and his kiss artistic, deliciously wanton and loving.

One inch.

Kyle closed his eyes. Sara gazed at his eyelashes before her eyes started to close as well . . .

Half an inch.

Their breaths were mingling, their tongues itching to touch, their arms beginning to reach for each other . . .

You're the Viking slut all over again! said the little devil on Sara's right shoulder, who had apparently returned after she brushed him off.

Sara blinked and wiped her bottom lip, as if she were the one with the cognac smear. "Wow," she said, "this stuff is amazing. Did we just live a parallel life in Paris?"

"Yes. And it was great. Let's go back."

"I think my butt's asleep. Did I tell you I'm getting married?"

*

Crap!
*

And it's not really even the truth!
*

What the hell is a commitment ceremony anyway?
*

I think I'm drunk.
*

"I mean, I wanted to talk to you about taking a week off."

"Married? No, you didn't tell me anything about this."

"Not for a few months. I'll make sure I get everything done here before I go. To Hawaii."

"Hawaii."

"Yeah. I hear there's good surfing there."

"Not a problem," Kyle said and took another pull at the cognac. "I trust you to carry your weight."

"It's important, or I wouldn't do it now."

Kyle didn't say anything.

"Anyway . . . "

"Congratulations."

"Thanks," Sara said.

"By the way. We may have substantial backing on the way. Jack Crumb made me an offer."

"Oh. Great."

"We can hire more staff. Expand our client base. Move up production."

"Sounds good."

"Good. Well, let me help you up."

Kyle pulled Sara up with him. She was wobbly, and fell against his chest. For a moment she just stayed there and had the absurd notion she wanted to go to sleep just for five minutes.

"Sara?"

"Oh, what?"

"Okay, I'm taking you home. You can pick up your car tomorrow."

"Okay, Antoine."

"Who's Antoine?"

"That's your Parisian name."

Why don't we ever learn?

Sara sat at her kitchen table, waiting for Night to finish concocting his special hangover smoothie. She didn't want to know what was in it, but when she saw him get a carton of eggs from the fridge, she said, "No raw eggs. Unless you want me to puke right here. And I won't clean it up."

"Okay babe. No eggs."

While swallowing bile, Sara pondered the absurdity of paying twenty-five hundred dollars for a hangover.

She was never going to drink again.

Never.

Right.

"Who's Antoine?" Night asked, as he threw a banana in the blender.

Sara stared at him. It hurt to think. Antoine? Oh . . . Antoine.

*

Crap!

*

"Why?"

"You were mumbling the name in your sleep."

Sara rested her aching head in her hands. Karma totally sucked.

"Antoine is a character in a script I'm writing," she hedged, "for French cognac."

"Never had cognac. Hey, a friend of mine is passing through. Would you mind if she stays with us?"

Sara raised her head. "Who?"

"Crystal. A friend of mine from—"

"Tahoe."

"Yeah. You'll like her."

"We don't have an extra bedroom anymore, with my office set up."

"No problem babe. She can sleep on the sofa.

Sara gritted her teeth while holding her aching head. She was fairly certain she was not going to like Crystal at all.

PART XI
The wedding reception

An unwanted houseguest lingers

S ara adjusted her dress. She was determined to look her very best. She had started getting ready for Greg and Brittney's wedding reception four hours ago. (She categorically refused to attend the gag-me-with-a-spoon wedding ceremony.) Actually, she had started getting ready weeks ago with a series of facials, peels, and dental bleaching. She had purchased an obscenely expensive eye cream. She had starved herself and lost one-quarter of an inch from her waistline, but nothing from her thighs.

*

Sigh . . .

*

She heard Night and Crystal laughing in the living room. Crystal was twenty-something. She had been sleeping on the sofa for days and days.

And days.

Crystal was an affront to any woman over thirty. No part of Crystal's body had begun to sag, bulge, or wrinkle. She had no gray hairs. Her thighs looked as though they belonged on a Barbie doll. She loved wheat grass juice. She knew how to campus on belay. She was always cheerful.

Sara loathed her.

Sara had begun smiling with her lips only. She wasn't at all sure she would ever be happy enough again to smile with her whole face.

This would prove helpful for avoiding those hideous crow's feet, now that the laser peel around her eyes had removed them.

Was it fair? Was it fair that Sara had to endure a cheerful, happy, thin, athletic, bohemian twenty-something girl in her face reminding her that she was not a cheerful, happy, thin, athletic, bohemian twenty-something girl?

Life was not fair. Karma was not fair. Sara was simply not going to pay any attention to either.

Instead, she would concentrate on her outfit.

She had decided to wear the expensive, white crinkly sheath she bought for Kyle's white party. She would adorn it with a gold bolero jacket full of bling she had spent another fortune on.

Sara's spending was completely out of control.

She didn't care, as long as she could have the liposuction. Nothing was going to stop her from having the cottage cheese sucked out of her thighs.

Back to the dress. The white sheath was also an act of rebellion. Sara knew it would irritate Brittney if she wore white, since presumably, the "bride" would be wearing white and would want to stand alone in her public farce of so-called purity and virginity.

Sara derived some pleasure from the thought of upstaging Brittney, which almost made her smile with her eyes.

Until she thought of Kyle, who was also invited to this gala event.

Sara and Kyle were back to speaking to each other in clipped sentences devoid of any emotion. In spite of their communication challenges, PopTrends seemed to be doing great. Apparently Kyle had lined up all sorts of deals and funding. Sara suspected it had something to do with Ever Vessence, the platinum-blonde bimbo, and her rich daddy.

Antoine would never compromise his ideals with a Hollywood-style two-digit-IQ bimbo, but evidently Kyle would.

Sara put the finishing touches to her hair. She was relieved that this was a good hair day. She looked fabulous in her outfit, her teeth gleamed, her plumped lips were pouting prettily, and her crow's feet were gone. She had no stray hairs beneath the bikini containment area.

So why did she still feel like dismembering Barbie dolls?

When Sara walked out of the bedroom, Night and Crystal were playing Xtreme skateboarding. Night looked roguish as usual in his baggy pants, loose tie, suit jacket and tennis shoes. Crystal was laughing and flinging her hair around, bouncing on the sofa.

"Am I interrupting recess?" Sara said. "Night, it's time to leave."

"You look babelicious, babe."

Sara resisted rolling her eyes to heaven.

"Great dress, Sara," Crystal chirruped. "Hey, thanks again for everything."

Sara smiled with her eyes only.

"Make yourself at home while we're gone," Sara told the unwanted houseguest.

And Night and Sara left for the wedding reception.

The truth will out

Sara walked into the huge ballroom at South Mountain Resort. Brittney had apparently hired an event planner. The room was decorated with props representing the faded elegance of Italy. Weather-worn statues, crumbling building fronts, a balcony, fake Italian cypress trees, cherubs festooned with roses pouring champagne . . .

Romeo and Juliet. How romantic. (On the other hand, how macabre, considering the tragic end to Shakespeare's story.) Sara had to appreciate the beauty of the scene, while at the same time suppressing her gag reflex.

She did notice, however, that her outfit blended swimmingly with the décor.

People were mingling about waiting for the happy couple to arrive. She noticed several ex-coworkers from T-Squared while Night procured drinks from the bar.

The classical Baroque music stopped and a blast of fanfare trumpets signaled everyone to pay attention. The happy couple appeared on the balcony, waving to their audience. Everyone cheered and applauded.

Greg took up a microphone and said, "Thank you all for coming.

Please help yourself to the food. There is no sit-down dinner, so eat, drink, and—"

Greg's eyes went to the entrance and everyone turned.

Sara's eyes narrowed. Kyle had entered with Ever. Ever was stunning in . . . a white dress! Sara gritted her teeth. As an afterthought, she was unable to categorize Ever's apparel as a dress. It was more like tight Swiss cheese: one spaghetti strap over the right shoulder, spandex ending at the upper thighs, and holes—one along the right side and one exposing a belly button which had some sort of bling attached to it.

"—eat, drink, and be married!" finished Greg after he retracted his drooling tongue.

Sara was too irritated at Ever's display of exhibitionism to pay any attention to Greg's ridiculous play on words.

"How could Kyle be with such a narcissistic exhibitionist?" Sara hissed. "How dare Ever upstage Brittney this way!"

"What babe?" Night said as he walked toward her with two martini glasses.

"Oh. Nothing. What is this?"

"It's called a *Negroni,* and you drink it before you eat. All I can remember is that there is gin in it. Oh, and vermouth, too."

Sara sipped. "It's a little bitter." She sipped again. "But I like it."

"Cheers babe," Night said. "To us."

Sara clinked glasses while staring at Kyle and his mating prize.

Antoine would never date such a shallow airhead, Sara thought. Just then, she noticed that Kyle was looking at her. They both looked away.

Sara also noticed Greg and Brittney approaching Kyle and Ever.

IImmmph, thought Sara. Brittney is kissing butt even at her own wedding.

"Crystal would love this," Night said as he looked around the room.

"Well, yeah," Sara said. "Crystal is so cheerful she would love a tax audit."

Night laughed. Apparently he did not take the comment as an insult.

The music changed to Tchaikovsky's *Romeo and Juliet* love theme. Greg and Brittney took their cue and started the first dance together. Guests moved aside to make more room.

Sara noticed that Brittney did not look all that happy.

Other couples joined the dancing newlyweds. Sara was disgusted to see Kyle twirl the fabulous Ever onto the dance floor.

Sara noticed that Kyle didn't look particularly happy either.

Night suggested they dance, but Sara told him she would rather have another drink. She suddenly felt an enormous urge to leave the reception and go to Bookaholic. She longed for a bottle of J. D., some sugared donuts, and racy conversation with Ash.

At the bar she ordered a shot and Night joined her.

"*Kanpai*," she said to her sort-of fiancé.

"*Okole maluna*," Night said, and clinked her glass.

Night was going on about Kahuna the surf god when Sara noticed Brittney belly up to the bar next to her. Brittney slammed down a shot as well. Then she asked for another. Sara was staring at her.

"Oh, Hi Sara," Brittney said. "You shouldn't have left me. I needed you."

Before Sara could answer—and it was taking her some time to do so, as her jaw had dropped slightly in surprise—Brittney shrugged her shoulders and walked away.

Weird wedding reception, Sara thought.

"What was that all about?" Night asked her.

"She was my boss when I quit T-Squared. She wanted me to wear suits and heels."

"You look great in heels babe."

Sara smiled at Night. He was so sweet, really. He seemed to like all women in general. Perhaps that wasn't such a great characteristic after all. Because at the moment, Kyle and Ever were walking over.

Actually, Ever wasn't walking. She was undulating over.

Sara pretended she didn't see them. She pointed to a cherub statue made to look weathered and tried to drag Night over to admire it.

"Wait," Night told her. "Hey Kyle. What's up, dude?"

Night extended his knuckles and the alpha male bumped them with his. The alpha male then introduced his mating prize.

Night charmingly took the mating prize's hand, and did not try to hide his appreciation.

Sara felt as though the smile on her face was possible only because there were millions of Lilliputians using tiny crowbars and scaffolding to prop her lips up.

"Hi Sara," the mating prize said. "Kyle talks about you all the time."

Sara was finding it difficult to disengage her lips from their fixed position in order to respond. She finally remembered that the mating prize, while well endowed with physical assets (some artificial), was sadly lacking in gray matter.

"That's because he admires my genius. Kyle keeps telling me how much he likes smart people."

"I know! Kyle and Daddy talk all the time about stuff I totally don't understand!"

"Oh, do they?" Sara noticed peripherally that Kyle was staring at her with thinned lips. She turned to him and asked, "So, what do you and Daddy talk about?"

"Business, right? Dude, that is one nice suit," said Night.

"Yeah," said Kyle. "Business." Sara and Kyle continued to stare at each other.

"And, hey, that is one smokin' hot dress," Night said to the mating prize.

Sara stopped trying to tell Kyle with her eyes that Antoine had more class than to date a ninety-eight-pound spoiled model with fake melons, and said to the ninety-eight-pound spoiled model with fake melons, "Oh, is that a dress? I thought it was a bathing suit. Just kidding!"

"I think I saw you in Sports, Illustrated. Are you a model?" Night asked.

"Yes," the mating prize said, smiling as widely as possible.

Sara tried not to squint from the glare. She was suddenly relieved that she had had her own teeth bleached. This made Sara smile widely as well.

"I was in issue six of two-thousand-fifteen, and issue one of two-thousand-sixteen."

Wooooooo! The mating prize rattled that off as though she actually knew some elementary math and how to read a calendar.

When Sara tilted her head, raised her eyebrows, fixed a clown smile on her face, and applauded in tiny little claps, Kyle excused himself and his mating prize to get drinks.

Sara noticed that both Brittney and Greg were watching them walk away. But then, Sara noticed that most people in the room were staring at the mating prize.

*

The slut!

*

Okay, so her name is Ever, not The Mating Prize.

*

Greg is such a horndog, thought Sara. He'll probably be fantasizing about Ever tonight on his honeymoon with his new wife. Sara was inclined to almost, but not quite, feel sorry for Brittney.

Night excused himself to visit the men's room. Sara fiddled with her nails, pretending that Kyle and Ever weren't there. Then, as melodrama is wont to beget more melodrama, she saw Ash, Andi, and Maddy arrive.

What were Ash and Maddy doing here? Andi was invited of course. Brittney had made sure everyone at T-Squared knew of her upcoming nuptials. Sara walked over to her friends.

Ash was looking particularly dashing, possibly due to the rakish grin, the ascot, and the casual way he wore his custom-tailored suit.

As Sara walked up, Ash opened his suit jacket and showed her the Barbie voodoo doll sticking out of an inside pocket. This was accompanied by an even crazier grin and a mischievous jigging of the eyebrows.

"Darling, you look fabulous. Kiss kiss."

"So do you, Ash. Did you actually comb your hair?"

"No."

"Hi Andi, Maddy."

"Hey," said Maddy, who was of course dressed in black. Apparently vampires simply could not dress in gay colors.

Andi just smiled.

"We got in on Andi's ticket," Ash told Sara. "You know I had to come." He flashed the Barbie again. "I couldn't leave Maddy home alone. So, one of us is gate-crashing, but I'm not sure which."

Sara was getting a sneaking suspicion that something odd was going on here. First of all, she had never seen Maddy outside the confines of the bookstore.

"Andi," Sara said, "have you found a new job yet?"

Andi looked at Maddy and Maddy nodded.

What the hell?

"No," Andi said, "but I have an interview Monday morning at Creative Printing. I'm sick of ad agencies."

"That's great. And how's Bry—Hans?"

"I'm sick of Hans, too. He's married. Everybody's married."

Ash began brushing invisible lint particles off his sleeves.

"Okay, well," Sara said, "anyway . . ."

Night walked up and greeted everyone. Sara told Ash to come with her to get some drinks, leaving the two women in Night's capable hands.

"What the bloody hell is going on here?" she asked Ash as soon as they were out of earshot.

"Darling, what do you mean?"

"You know what I mean."

"We British blokes are famous for our avoidance techniques. How am I doing?"

Sara glared at Ash with slits-for-eyes.

"May I have a word with you, Sara? Hello Ash," Kyle said.

Ash and Sara turned to face Kyle, who was glaring at Sara with slits-for-eyes.

"Of course," Ash said cheerily. "I'll just pop over to the dessert table and get something scrummy."

Kyle took a loose hold of Sara's elbow and led her to a semi-private spot beside a huge urn containing a fake Italian cypress.

Kyle leaned in and started to say something. Then he started again. Then his lips formed a thin line.

"Well," Sara finally said. "Spit it out before I die of old age. Your mating prize is waiting for you to return, so she doesn't have to keep a conversation going by herself. There are very few sentences completely comprised of one-syllable words."

"Why are you getting married?"

Thrown off balance by the question, Sara said, "Well, I'm not getting married as such."

"What does that mean?"

"Why are you dating Ever? Well, I suppose that's a stupid question. Why did you lie about dating Ever?"

"I didn't. Whenever I said I wasn't, I wasn't. And when I was it was because I had to."

"What does that mean?"

"Sara . . . I . . . we need to talk."

"We are talking."

Kyle was looking at Sara again with those eyes—eyes that were trying to tell her something.

"What was your French name?" he finally said, with a much lower, gentler tone.

"What?"

"Mine was Antoine. What was yours?"

Sara could not help the upturn of her lips, which incidentally were looking cushiony and pleasing in a beautiful shade of lipstick called "coral moon."

"Fleur."

"Flower," Kyle said.

They looked at each other and smiled.

"I wonder if they have any cognac at the bar," Kyle said.

"Not the kind that comes in a lead crystal bottle designed by a famous French artist, I'm sure."

Dust particles were swimming happily, even eagerly, in the glow of halogen lamps placed in the urn to up-light the Italian cypress.

"What happened to Antoine and Fleur? Did they live happily ever after?"

Sara lost her smile. "No. Antoine was swept away by a femme fatale of no consequence. Fleur was not pleased."

"Perhaps Antoine didn't know that Fleur really cared."

"Perhaps. But that's not how the story goes," Sara said with some agitation.

"Kyle, there you are," said Ever as she came bee-bopping up.

Sara and Kyle backed away from each other as Ever slipped her arm through Kyle's. "I'm dying to dance," she said.

Good, die, thought Sara.

The dance floor was getting full as Dean Martin sang, *Everybody loves somebody sometime* . . .

Sara went back to Ash, Maddy, and Andi. She asked where Night was.

"Um, darling," Ash told her, " Night got a call and had to leave. He couldn't find you to tell you."

Sara looked at her cell. It was dead. Bollocks.

"Call from who?"

"Whom."

"Whom then! From whom?"

"Someone named Crystal."

Andi looked at Sara as if to say, Who is Crystal and why didn't you tell me about her?

Maddy was staring at Sara with vampire stillness.

"Crystal!" Sara said. "What did she want?"

"Apparently she had some kind of emergency . . . video game took a shite or something."

*

What the f**k?

*

Crystal is such a pain in the wazoo!

*

"He said he would come back as soon as possible," Ash added. "Has anybody noticed that Gimpy isn't gimpy anymore?"

Sara seethed into the middle distance, where she was picturing Night helping out Crystal with her little freaking emergency.

"I need a drink," she said, and headed for the bar.

When she got to the bar, she discovered that the ménage à trois had followed her.

That was it! "Ménage à trois," she said flatly to the three of them.

"Not exactly darling, but yes, that too," Ash said.

It was then that Sara noticed the black choker Andi was wearing, which really did not go with the flower print dress and crimson jacket with the collar turned up.

Then Sara noticed that the choker looked more like a collar.

Then Sara noticed that the collar matched the belt Maddy was wearing.

Then Sara noticed that Andi's cheeks were pink and that Maddy was becoming so still she was corpse-like.

"Andi, what are you holding?" Sara asked.

"It's a chain," Maddy said out of the stillness, which startled Sara so much she flinched, "attached to her collar."

Ash was grinning wickedly. "They had to disconnect to come in here. What would people think?"

"Andi's being topped," Maddy told Sara, with eyes that said, This is my gig, bitch.

"Topped?"

Ash said, "Let's dance. We British blokes come fully trained from boarding school with excellent dancing skills."

Sara suffered herself to be led by Ash onto the dance floor, but she kept stealing glances at Maddy and Andi.

Andi looked embarrassed, but in a strange way, happy.

Sara thought her head might explode any minute, and that would simply not be pretty on her expensive white dress. What was Crystal playing at? Visions of dominatrix outfits on Maddy filled her mind. What had Kyle been trying to tell her? What the hell was a commitment ceremony?

"Okay," Ash said as he guided Sara across the dance floor, "if you must know all the sordid details . . ."

Sara, while attempting to prevent her head from exploding, had the presence of mind to notice how well Ash danced.

"My dear wife is a bit of a Domme."

"Goes with the vampire lifestyle, I suppose."

"Well, darling, perhaps. But some very normal dishy ladies and blokes indulge . . . including yours truly."

"You're not normal," Sara reminded him.

"Yes I am."

"No you're not."

"Am too."

"Are not."

"And dear Andi, well, she is a perfect sub."

"And what part do you play?"

"I'm a switch, darling. I can go either way. I'm just in it for the sex. We three seem to be getting along swimmingly." Ash winked.

"Horndog."

"Listen love. Life is short. Have fun while you're here, and all that sort of rubbish."

"You sound like Bryan."

"That wanker."

"Aren't you being a bit of a hypocrite?"

"Well . . ." Ash grinned wickedly.

Ash twirled Sara and she almost bumped into Kyle. Sara noticed that Ever was smiling at her with her lips only. What was that about?

Greg showed up and tapped Kyle on the shoulder for a dance with Ever. Kyle bowed out and stood on the periphery near the potted cypress. Sara noticed that he was looking at her.

She also noticed that Ever was looking at Kyle. Greg was looking at Ever, or more accurately, drooling at her. And Brittney was looking at Greg.

"Ash, can I borrow your cell phone?" Sara wanted to call Night and find out if he had satisfied Crystal yet.

"Here, darling. Just don't read the text messages, they're not fit for innocent eyes."

Sara grabbed the cell phone and looked for a quiet place to make the call. She stopped at the bar and downed a shot.

Sara felt her knotted muscles loosen a bit, and she headed for the powder room.

Once in the posh powder room, which consisted of a lovely sitting area and a bathroom beyond that, Sara breathed a sigh of relief. She called Night.

"Hey babe. Where were you? I looked all over for you."

"You couldn't have looked that hard."

"We're having a problem with the video game."

"I know. Ash told me about the dire emergency."

"I'll be back as soon as I can. Oh hey, this cable is in the wrong port!"

"Oh, cool!" Sara heard Crystal say, "maybe that's it!"

"Far out," said Night. "Let's see if it works now."

"Night, you are so sweet to do this," said Crystal.

Sara just stood there listening to the The Peanut Gallery until she had heard enough.

"Night," Sara said, "Night. Hey, Night!"

"Hey babe. Looks like we—"

"You know what? Stay home. I'll catch a ride back with Ash in his old fogy van. I don't want to stay much longer anyway."

"Okay, babe. See you when you get home. Love you."

Sara ended the call and stewed for a while. She could almost feel steam issuing from her ears.

*

Crystal. The sneaky slut!

*

Night was sweet. Too sweet. Too sweet to the likes of a pretty little interloper with no fat cells and enough cheerfulness to gag Mother Teresa.

Crystal was a silly, sophomoric girl with no real life experience, who had filled out an application to work at the climbing gym.

Sara went to the mirror. She admired her look as she replenished her lipstick—so much more sophisticated and classy than a bouncing sophomore could ever achieve. She was a business partner in a viable business. She felt . . . accomplished. It occurred to her that Night was miles from where she was. All he cared about was Kahuna the surf god. No wonder he and Crystal got along so well.

Sara decided she was not going home anytime soon just to babysit the two of them.

Some faint sounds reached Sara's ears while she perfected her coiffure. As she quietly walked back to the bathroom, she heard discreet little snivels.

Protruding from an ornate, pink and gold stall door, was the hem of a wedding dress.

"Brittney?" Sara said.

The sniveling stopped.

"Brittney, is that you in there?"

"Yeah," said Brittney, "almost done."

Sara heard nose-blowing, and Brittney emerged smiling and smoothing her dress.

"Is everything okay?" Sara asked. Brittney did not look okay. Her eyes were red-rimmed, her mascara was smudged, her face was blotchy, and she looked generally pathetic.

"I'm fine," she said, and promptly broke into sobs.

Sara's heart caved at this point, overriding all resentments hitherto held for the kiss-ass designer, and went out sympathetically to the fellow female.

She went to Brittney and put a protective arm around her shoulders.

"Come in here and sit down," she told Brittney, as she led her into the sitting area. She then threw the bolt shut on the door so no one else could get in.

Brittney sat in an overstuffed pink chair with gold trim, and pulled pink tissues from the box next to it.

Sara pushed her chair closer to Brittney and said, "Now tell me what's going on."

"I look hideous. How am I going to go back out there?"

"I have makeup in my purse. We'll fix that." Sara was always prepared for emergency redo's.

Brittney dried her eyes. "My face is broken out. I gained ten pounds, all on my ass. Just in time for my wedding! The most important day of my life! Waaaa-haaaaa-haaaaaaaaaa."

Holy crap! Sara thought. The Barbie voodoo doll!

"And now, Greg! He can't take his eyes off that blonde bimbo Kyle brought. Waaa-haaaa-haaaaaaaaa."

This was a dilemma. Greg certainly was acting like a dog after a bitch in heat. This would probably not be a good time to mention spankme2nite.

"Brittney, Greg wanted to marry you, which means he must love you."

Brittney looked at Sara. "Yeah, I guess he does."

"He doesn't care about a few pimples that are going to go away within a week."

"Yeah, I guess you're right."

"Let's go fix your face," Sara said. "You'll be amazed at what I have in my little bag of tricks."

While at the mirror, Sara helped Brittney out with concealer, mascara, and a choice of three lovely shades of lipstick. She also had clear nail polish in case Brittney had any nylon snags.

"How dare that little bitch wear a dress like that to my wedding?" Brittney said as they were choosing a lipstick shade. "You look nice," Brittney added with a slight frown.

"Thank you," Sara said, as she glanced in the mirror. It was true; she looked fabulous. In fact, compared to Brittney's pathetic situation, Sara's life was a piece of chocolate fudge cake.

"Don't pay any attention to Ever," Sara told Brittney. "She's not worth your notice. She has had everything handed to her on a silver spoon, including her fake boobs. You, on the other hand, are a self-made woman, who is smart, professional, and gorgeous. The guys at T-Squared were always checking you out, even Mr. T."

Brittney smiled.

"Would you want to trade places with the likes of Ever? She probably can't even spell the word wedding."

Brittney considered this and said, "No. You're right, I wouldn't."

"Damn straight," Sara said.

"It figures Kyle would have a girlfriend like that speaking of silver spoons," Brittney said. "And Mrs. T always was jealous of me, the Viking bitch!"

Sara looked up at Brittney in the mirror.

"What do you mean, Viking bitch?"

"The T. stands for Teterson as you know, which is the Americanized spelling of T-e-i-t-u-r-s-s-o-n. They were originally from Iceland. So Mrs. T truly is the ice queen."

"Iceland? Viking?" Sara just stood there. Then she stood there some more.

Her mind was in turmoil. Her mental cogs were turning. There were butterflies in her stomach. The galaxy was spinning. The universe was expanding. And the dust particles were whirling in anticipation.

"You look great now," Sara said to Brittney. Then to her absolute surprise, she kissed Brittney on the cheek.

Brittney said thank you and glowed brightly from Sara's help, her kindness, and her kiss, as she watched Sara fly out of the room.

A little friendly advice

Sara left the powder room to find Ash. She needed to speak with him as soon as possible.

After scouring the reception, she went outside where the smokers were gathered. She saw her three friends and rushed over, taking fast little steps so she didn't fall off her high heels.

Maddy was wielding a cigarette holder with vampire-like gravity.

Andi smiled at Sara. Now that Sara's heart had melted in the powder room, she kissed Andi on the cheek, too, knowing that her sweet friend needed it.

Maddy, however, was not pleased.

"Ash," Sara said, "come here." She dragged Ash aside and tried to begin.

What poured out was mostly incomprehensible.

"Bloody hell," said Ash.

"Damn straight," said Sara. "What am I going to do?"

"Okay, love. Let me see if I understand," Ash said. "You thought Gimpy was your soulmate. But now you think that Kyle might be your soulmate. But you have agreed to marry Gimpy to balance your karma. But you're afraid you will be making more karma by marrying the wrong Viking?"

"Gimpy, I mean Night, might not be the Viking at all. Don't you see? Maybe it's really Kyle. Oh jeez! I was trying to make it all fit."

Ash put his hands on Sara's shoulders and looked into her frantic eyes. "Listen, darling. Take a deep breath. Which soulmate candidate do you love?"

Sara thought about this.

"I mean really love," Ash added.

There are many types of love, thought Sara. She found that answering this question was difficult. When she really, really thought about it, she loved almost everybody, which was an amazing realization since she thought she hated almost everything.

"Don't settle," Ash said. "That's what I did. I sold out to dear Uncle Edmund, and now I dither my way through life with a ball and chain of my own making. Not that I mind," and he winked, "it's quite brilliant at times, actually."

Sara smiled at him affectionately.

"Don't settle," Ash repeated.

Sara looked back at the door into the reception. Then remembered to tell Ash about the Barbie voodoo doll.

"That's right," she said, "pimples, and ten pounds on the butt. We need to de-voodoo those dolls."

"I'd better find out if Andi is still in touch with that wanker, Bryan," Ash said. "He may be having a few problems of his own."

Sara looked back toward the door again.

She saw Kyle and Ever coming out.

Sara did not hesitate now.

She ran over to them in fast little steps, ever mindful not to fall off her heels, clutching her purse, and looking for all intents and purposes like a little girl who had discovered a hidden box of chocolates, but wasn't sure she was allowed to eat any of them.

Kyle broke into a smile at her approach. Ever smiled with her lips only.

"Are you leaving?" Sara asked.

Ever said, yes, and Kyle said, no, at the same time.

"I'd like to speak with you about something, Kyle," Sara said.

Ever's smile faded to slits-for-eyes.

"Business?" Kyle asked.

"Business," Sara said. "And it might take a while."

Kyle handed Ever the keys to his BMW. "Ever, go ahead and take my car home. I may be a while."

"But—" Ever began.

"It's okay," Kyle told Ever. "I'll pick it up tomorrow." And he pushed her gently toward his car.

"Daddy isn't going to like this," she whined.

But Kyle had ceased to pay any attention to Ever, and was gazing at Sara.

Moonbeams were bathing them both in gorgeous soft light, and millions of moonlit dust particles were swimming excitedly around them, singing little love ditties.

"What business do you want to talk about?" Kyle asked, as he led Sara off to a private bench surrounded by palm trees and potted petunias. "Where's Night?"

"He went home," Sara told him. She was glad to be sitting considering her wobbly legs and tingling innards.

"Oh," Kyle said, as though that one-syllable word had a whole paragraph of meaning.

"Are your parents Vikings?" Sara asked. "I mean, are they from Iceland?"

"Yes," said Kyle, puzzled at the question. "But it's funny you say Viking. My mother goes to psychics, and she has been told that I was a—"

"—Viking in a past life," Sara finished for him.

They drew closer. They were also holding hands, but hadn't quite realized it yet.

"That's right," Kyle said. "How did you know that?"

"I was told I was a Viking's wife. This seems like a strange coincidence," Sara said.

"There are no coincidences. That's what my mother tells me."

"I like your mother."

Ash was watching the two of them from afar. As Maddy directed their little group to leave, Ash blew an unseen kiss to Sara.

"Kyle, about my upcoming marriage . . . which, really wasn't a marriage but a commitment ceremony, which I really didn't—"

"Yes? What about it?"

"I've decided not to go through with it. Night's a great guy. But I think I was settling."

"Settling for what?"

"The wrong Viking."

They moved a bit closer to each other.

"So who is the right Viking?" Kyle asked.

"I think you know the answer to that question."

"Tell me anyway."

They gazed at each other through a haze of moonbeams and dancing dust particles. A protective veil had lifted, and here they were, looking into each other's eyes for the first time without it.

"You are," she said.

Kyle smiled. His smile was full of everything a smile could be: handsomeness, charisma, bliss, happiness, and something more. He had become the little boy, with rocks and sticks in his pockets, wanting to be loved, and finding out that he was.

Their lips, unbeknownst to either of them, had decided on their own to begin the slow descent into union.

Sara felt her eyes closing. She felt their breaths mingling. She felt, finally, the sweet, utterly delicious sensation of Kyle's kiss.

Sara heard a chorus of angels singing somewhere.

Their lips were long-lost friends, finally reunited after centuries of waiting. Why bother rating such a kiss—it was off the charts.

Sara swooned. Kyle let his passion spill over Sara in waves of ecstasy.

Melodramatic? Yes. But, oh, so wonderfully enchanting.

When they finally emerged from their flight to lip-nirvana, Kyle grabbed Sara and held her tightly. Sara held him tightly.

Oh, the glory of karma! Oh, the magic of true love!

"We don't have a car, or any way to get home," Sara finally said.

Kyle answered after laying down a velvet path of karmic kisses on Sara's neck.

"I'll have someone pick us up."

Kyle made a call, and turned his attention back to his love, Sara of the cottage cheese thighs. Sara of the witty comebacks. Sara of the intense gaze and impish smile.

"When did you know?"

Kyle knew exactly what she meant.

"I'm not sure. I resisted it for a long time. Falling in love with you was not in my plan."

"Mine either." Sara said. "Things never turn out the way I think they will."

"Screw plans. When you go with the flow great things happen," Kyle said.

"Just look at Antoine and Fleur and what happened when they lost their passports. I've changed the ending by the way. They did live happily ever after."

*

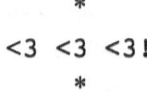

*

Following several enraptured minutes of more soulmate kissing, petting, expressions of amazement, and tender endearments, the limo arrived.

Kyle led Sara to the limo, where the driver was holding the door open for them. There was a bottle of cognac in the back instead of champagne.

They snuggled into the seat, and the driver tipped his hat and closed the door. What happened next was beyond what mere words could describe.

PART XII
Sara's fortieth birthday

A little bed and breakfast in the Latin Quarter

Sara poured French roast into little china cups edged with gold. She buttered a freshly baked croissant and held it up to Kyle's lips.

He took a bite and told her it was *délicieux*.

Everything was delicious . . . their room, the balcony they were sitting on, the French Quarter, the smell of coffee, and the fact that they were here in Paris for Sara's birthday in honor of Antoine and Fleur.

Kyle hadn't brushed his hair yet and neither had Sara. The marvel of this was that she had never looked so beautiful, or Kyle so handsome.

Sara's robe had fallen away from her thighs, her cottage cheese thighs, which looked so fetching in France, yet had seemed so hideous in the Hollywoodized U.S. She might be a lovely woman in a Toulouse-Lautrec painting, lounging at the Moulin Rouge.

They were situated on the *Rue Mouffetard*, where students and philosophers debated at sidewalk cafes, where bohemian boutiques and used book shops abounded (Ash would have loved it), and where lovers roamed, wrapped in sunshine and showered with scents from fresh-flower sellers.

Kyle reached for a lock of Sara's hair, which was loose and wavy, in typical Fleur-fashion. He asked her what she wanted to do today.

Sara sighed luxuriously. Everything seemed so far away and insignificant, yet perfect, as if the whole world had stopped while she and her soulmate drank each other in to the last drop in Paris. She thought of their growing business back home, PopTrends. They had hired staff, in spite of Jack Crumb's withdrawal of support. She thought of Night, who was consoling himself with Crystal. She thought of her future with Kyle, and where it might lead. She decided she didn't want to do anything. For now, just being was nice. This moment was perfect.

"Maybe we could walk around later and find a spot to drink wine, and listen to a French singer with a throaty voice lamenting about lost love."

Kyle pulled Sara over to sit on his lap.

"You'll never, ever lose my love."

Sara smiled the smile of deep contentment. Could things get any better?

Kyle pulled something from his robe pocket. It was a box. He said, "Happy birthday, *mon amour*."

Sara looked at the box. The box looked back.

"For pity's sake," said the box, "stop gaping and open me up!"

Sara ignored the box and looked at Kyle.

"Open it," he said.

Sara opened the box. She caught her breath. It was a gorgeous emerald ring. It looked vintage. Sara thought Kyle must have been a magician to have purchased it, as they had been glued to each others' sides while browsing the boutiques.

"It was my grandmother's. Then my mother's. It came with her from Iceland. It's yours now. My mother believes you are my past-life Viking wife, so she passed the ring on willingly. No strings attached."

Sara stared at the beautiful gift with a full heart, mindful of the honor bestowed.

"But, it should stay in the family," Sara said.

"Mother has no daughters. And she thinks you are family. Soul family."

Sara put the ring on. It was a perfect fit, of course, as karma, soul families, and true love would have it.

"But if you say yes, it can be more than just a gift."

Sara said, "What do you mean?"

"I think you know what I mean."

"Say it anyway."

Kyle smiled and said, "Marry me?"

~ For Powder, a true love if ever there was one. ~

Free Ebook

If you've ever had a fat cell you didn't like, this book's for you. From holiday fat challenges to summer bathing suit blues, it's a sweet (as in sugary), bumpy ride.

Go to authordlfisher.com/free-ebook/ to download your free copy of *The Fat Chronicles.* **:-)**